WATCHING AND WAITING

Lee watched them from the brush.

He'd learned a few things.

The men were not bad with their weapons. They were not particularly great with them either but he'd have to be careful.

The dog hadn't spooked them. Nor had they worried about an owner possibly being nearby. So they did not feel in any danger. Perhaps it was their firepower, maybe their numbers. He'd seen it before. You got lucky for a while so you got complacent. So complacent that before too long a single man could walk right round your camp at night and turn every claymore inward so that when they fired, they fired right at you, right in your faces, not at the enemy. Your own mines killed you.

Then he'd tossed the snake and the woman had acted well and promptly. Okay. He would not underestimate her.

He slid off into the brush, back a few yards to where the dog waited.

It was dusk.

Tonight, he thought. A little later.

To use the complacency. To have most of them sleeping. To do it the old way, under the stars.

He felt filled with a burning manic energy and younger then he had in years. The weariness of the past few days was gone.

He felt almost like whistling. Later there would be wariness, danger, maybe even terror. Now there was the excitement of knowing what was coming and knowing in your gut what you were here to do...

JACK KETCHUM

COVER

LEISURE BOOKS   NEW YORK CITY

A LEISURE BOOK®

June 2009

Published by

Dorchester Publishing Co., Inc.
200 Madison Avenue
New York, NY 10016

ISBN 10: 0-8439-6187-2
ISBN 13: 978-0-8439-6187-4

Visit us on the web at www.dorchesterpub.com.

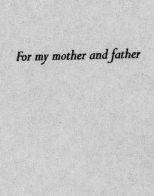

For my mother and father

COVER

FOREWORD

What did you do during the war, daddy?
by Jack Ketchum

I don't have any children that I know of, but if I did and they asked me the above I'd have to say *a lot* and then *hell, not much.*

In 1961 when the first United States support troops were arriving in Vietnam I was a sophomore in high school with little on my mind other than rock 'n' roll, girls, more girls, still *more* girls and Elvis' performance with Tuesday Weld in WILD IN THE COUNTRY. The words *war in Southeast Asia* were on nobody's tongue back then so I wasn't alone in my *apres-50s* innocence.

Three years later I went off to college and all of that had changed. Johnson had finagled the Tonkin Gulf Resolution through Congress and the wise-ass kid from New Jersey who just barely managed the last-minute grades to get *into* college was working like a demon to stay there. Dean's List. President of His Class. Member of this Club and that Club. Singing for his supper and tuition money—sounding a little *like* Elvis truth be told—by night and emptying rich Boston matrons' garbage cans by day.

Anything to stay out of the cold, cold draft.

By the time of the Tet Offensive in 1968, when an estimated 34,000 souls gave up the ghost in just ten days and a thoroughly discredited LBJ's subsequent declaration that he *warn't runnin' fer no durn reelection* I had metamorphosized once more. Into a colorful tie-dyed bell-bottomed beaded bearded freak with hair longer than the painted Jaysus on Oral Roberts' bedroom wall. I was doped-out and LSD'd and in love with a woman who shot crystal meth into her arm. I marched and demonstrated. I Made Love Not War. One memorable night in Cambridge the police in full riot gear chased me into, through, and out again of a Hayes-Bickford cafeteria.

I was faster in those days.

The invasion of Cambodia found four of us crossing the country from New York to San Francisco on a pilgrimage to Where it All Began. Summers I'd been acting in a Maine summer-stock company playing El Gallo and Duperret and Mack the Knife and I had just finished two years teaching high school—and warring with the faculty, the School Board and the local PTA. There were no Flowers in my Hair but there *was* my father's beat-up pushed-in grey fedora which went nicely with the love-beads and granny-glasses.

My first writing job, doing soft-sell ad copy for the *Psychology Today* Book Club, began out there and did not immediately turn me into a Fucking Suit. We stayed on the coast until wintertime and then flew back to New York City. At LAX I was arrested for carrying a nickle-bag of pot and four black beauties in my chamois aviator jacket and then released when a Mexican businessman's pocketed .38 set the metal detectors screaming.

Maybe I was luckier in those days too.

It took until 1975 for South Vietnam to collapse finally and by that time I *was* a Fucking Suit, working as an agent and glorified secretary for the Cosmodemonic Literary Agency—Scott Meredith, Inc. I was one year away from quitting that, on the hunch that if I could sell some of the shit I was peddling I could sell my own crude offal as well. It worked out. I shed the suit forever in favor of a bathrobe and an IBM Selectric I could almost get to by simply rolling out of bed.

The point of all this is not so much what I *did* do but what I didn't.

I didn't go to war.

I knew a few Boys who did. One was a roommate of mine who dropped out freshman year to join the Marines. As kids we used to haunt the double-bill nudie shows in Boston's Combat Zone—THE IMMORAL MR. TEAS and ORGY AT LIL'S. We used to have a fine old time. I bumped into him years later on the streets of New York. It was during my longhair days and he wasn't glad to see me.

Another shared my first apartment on Beacon Hill, completed his B.A. and then enlisted in the Army. He thought it was only right. Almost two years later I was still in Boston teaching and he came to visit me on leave, sat sobbing on my couch and told me that I was the first person stateside who'd truly welcomed him, that most people were treating him like a goddamn war criminal, that he felt betrayed by all of us back home and betrayed by the Army too. He'd been shot—not a critical wound but quite sufficient to scare the shit out of him and the Army had made him an offer. He was short, with just a few months to go. He could do one of two things. He could reenlist for another hitch and have a nice cozy desk job behind a typewriter or he could go back to the *villes* and firefights and serve out the remainder of his tour. My friend chose the desk job and I'm glad he did. I hope he is too.

I've seen him a few times since though, and I wish I could be sure.

There's nobody in my generation of U.S. citizens who doesn't know somebody—or for that matter, hasn't lost somebody—in that goddamn war. And I doubt that there's a writer of my generation who hasn't wanted to address the subject in one way or another

Arguably it's better if you were there. For the writing part I mean.

You get the sounds right, the feels right, the *sweats* right.

But this little piggy stayed home . . .

The idea for my own stab at a Vietnam novel arrived full-blown in the form of a fifteen-minute segment—or a *segment* of that segment—of HBO's hour-long documentary series AMERICA UNDERCOVER. The title, now that I think of it, may have derived from there too. The film was about Vietnam vets attempting to adjust—and mostly failing to adjust—to life back home in The World. It profiled four men in various places and situations and one of them was this guy living way out in the woods because in town he was dangerous to others, he couldn't control the flashbacks and the rages. He'd tear apart a bar or a workplace. Out here he was only dangerous to himself maybe. And maybe to his wife.

Twenty-one years have passed since then, twenty since I wrote the book so I don't remember the specifics very well but I do remember that this guy really got to me. His struggle with himself got to me and so did his solution to his problem—his voluntary isolation. A jail as big as the sky.

He didn't want to hurt anybody anymore.

More than that, his *wife* got to me. Here's a woman, I thought, with a major problem and she's no dope, she damn well knows it. She's living with this man at intense personal risk. He goes off, he's dangerous as Friendly Fire. Yet if she leaves him she's morally certain he'll die out here. One of these days he'll eat his rifle.

I told him once that if he killed himself I didn't want to be the one to find him . . . but who else is there? I will find him. I will be the one. I know it.

I believe those lines are taken almost directly from her real words in the film.

She loves him. *Adores* him. It's written all over her.

And she broke my heart for all their pain and made me mad at the war all over again.

The woman appears only very briefly in the book but to my way of thinking she informs the entire thing, sets its tone and in her very absence provides its theme. *No se puede vivir sin amar.* The Malcolm Lowry line which introduces the novel. *It is not possible to live without love.*

I wanted to write a book about a guy who has to try to do just that.

A loveless Vietnam transposed to a loveless forest back here in The World. A haunted aching loneliness almost beyond imagining.

And back in high school my dad said I had no ambition.

I *had* to imagine it. It was my *job* to imagine it.

The other characters, from the worlds of publishing, theatre, fashion—those I thought I could handle. Hell, I'd been an agent. I'd *dated* a female bodybuilder for months for god's sake. I'd known the pangs of my own plays being relegated to off-off-Broadway black-box theatres. I'd even climbed a mountain with Norman Mailer once with a ROLLING STONE photographer trailing right along behind. The magazine published the photos so I have proof.

But as to the vet, the centerpiece of my story— well, *I simply wasn't there.*

So what did *I* know?

I needed help and needed it big-time. I was not about to rip off the vets with some fancy literary footwork and a little reading. If it came down to that I wouldn't write the damn thing at all.

Help, for me, was Richard Carey.

I met Dick through a mutual friend, Neil Linden, who worked with his wife Pat in a hospital speech therapy unit.

A lot of vets won't talk to you about the war and with good reason. They want to try to put its horrors behind them once and for all and get on with life. Some won't even discuss it among one another let alone to some writer-type civilian stranger. I don't blame them. My ex-roommate, the one who'd been blackmailed into reupping in the Army, was the first I called. He explained to me politely but firmly that he'd said all he had to say about the war on my couch that day.

Dick, on the other hand, *liked* to talk.

Not that it was always easy. Over the course of our many conversations I saw him wipe away more than a few stray tears. I think it's lucky Dick can cry. I think a lot of the guys who get into serious trouble can't.

Talking, for Dick, was clearly a kind of therapy but it was also more than that. There are vets who seem to have lived whole lifetimes of experience in that war and having done two hitches Dick was one of them. This wasn't just therapy. He was describing a personal history to me. A history he knew had importance and weight beyond his own feelings. He remembered the war vividly, both the bad and the good—yes, there *is* a little heaven in a disaster area and I learned that too—but he had no illusions about which was which. He was candid and spared himself nothing.

From his notes:

Sgt. Byerling on second tour . . . became our demo expert, carried a lot of C-4 and blasting caps. Hit grenade booby trap and was blown into six pieces all over the place, beautiful and balmy day, like walking in the park . . . went south, joined the 11th Cavalry . . . set up night ambush. I killed the VC point, two others killed, others escaped . . . three ducks KIA (Killed In Action) and relished with apricot jam . . . choppered west . . . patrolled deep into jungles . . . misty, rainy, damp . . . leech valley, *everyone had them . . . returned to camp with heavily fortified sandbagged bunkers, monsoon hit us full force and severely damaged all bunkers, two guys got broken legs when the walls caved in, fun city . . . moved north . . . new guys in unit couldn't kill VC girl with rifle . . . she escaped . . . Thanksgiving Day, 1967, slight drizzle . . . received word Cav unit in trouble . . . two platoons lined up for chopper pickup . . . choppers came in the wrong way and landed in hell . . . first two choppers shot down on the ground, second platoon practically wiped out . . .*

Just a sample.

From his wife Pat I learned what it's like to live with and love a man who is still haunted by what he'd seen and done In Country. A man you still have to wake up carefully and quietly lest he think he's Back There and goes for your throat. A man who will still get shaky at the sound of helicopters overhead and flinches thinking *incoming* at pretty much any loud noise.

Dick turned me on to a lot of books, articles and novels on the subject too. Michael Herr's DISPATCHES, Boettecher's VIETNAM· THE VALOR AND THE SORROW, Goldman and Fuller's CHARLIE COMPANY, Richard Hammer's ONE MORNING IN THE WAR, Ron Kovic's BORN ON THE FOURTH OF JULY, Tim O'Brien's GOING AFTER CACCIATO, John M. Del Vecchio's THE THIRTEENTH VALLEY to name a few.

The books all helped but it was mostly Dick and Pat. They would tell me stories all night long if I wanted over beers and scotches, at cookouts and in restaurants, welcomed me into their home time after time over the course of several months and allowed me to ask anything at all, however personal, any time, day or night, on the phone or in person. I've never before or since had such generous collaboration. Or collaborators who were so much fun to be with. I thanked them both in the Warner edition. But I think that a whole lot of the voice in this book is *Dick's* voice—rereading it today I hear him clearly—and I'm grateful for the opportunity to thank both him and Pat again and at a little more length.

It took me almost a year to get up the nerve to start writing COVER, to feel that I had my vet right. Once I did it came smoothly over about a six-month period, with the help of a lot more phone consultations with Dick and Pat to make sure I got the details down, a little fashion advice from other sources and a few tutorials from an old buddy on how to plant, cultivate and harvest large thriving quantities of *cannibis sativa*. My agent, Alice Martell, was able to sell the book fairly quickly to Jim Frost at Warner Books. By April of '86 I'd signed the contract.

Frost was enthusiastic. Since the novel was clearly my most mainstream to date—some would say it still is—Jim wanted it to be my first hardcover, my *breakthrough* novel. So did the brass at Warner.

At least initially.

Among the many other things Vietnam should have taught us was not to put too much faith in the brass.

When the Powers That Be at Warner started backpeddling on the book—they probably saw the sales-figures for HIDE AND SEEK, which might have scared off the hardiest of souls—and informed Jim that they actually saw it more as a paperback original than a hardcover title Jim responded with regret but told me we were still in good shape. He could estimate a print-run of 230,000 copies.

Not bad, I thought. That's not bad at all. I could even make a little cash here.

But would I mind changing the title to STALKING GROUND?

I did.

I did mind. I thought STALKING GROUND was lame as hell and had nothing to do with the heart of the book but only its surface plotting. STALKING GROUND was a sensationalist bullshit title designed to betray the vets. And my guy wasn't so much stalking people as he was at war with them, protecting his own butt, which was what you *did* in war. COVER was far more suitable I argued. Everybody *in* the book's seeking cover, metaphorically speaking, in one way or another. The vet, his wife, Kelsey, Ross—the whole damn cast of characters. We pushed and pulled over this for quite a while. In the end I won.

And probably I lost too.

Because the book did not get a print-run of 230,000. The run was more like 40,000. The same kind of run Ballantine gave HIDE AND SEEK. And Warner slapped cover art on the book which was geared to the title STALKING GROUND anyway—a bunch of civilians running through the forest away from a leering sneering soldier.

Buried again.

I rarely saw it anywhere on the stands. It received

no reviews that I know of other than one from Chas Balun in DEEP RED. By the end of the year the only place on earth it seemed to exist for some weird reason was in Talahassee, Florida. Ann Kennedy of THE SILVER WEB kept sending me dog-eared copies from there or I'd have none to this day.

Up till now.

What did you do during the war, daddy.

A lot and hell, not much. Not compared to the vets anyway. All the morphings I mentioned at the beginning of this piece, sure. Chasing high school girls, getting wasted, acting, singing, protesting, traveling, teaching.

And one other thing. Through it all I was writing. Or trying to write. From early high school on.

—Jack Ketchum, September, 1999

Let us keep courage and try to be patient and gentle. And not mind being eccentric, and make distinction between good and evil.

—Vincent van Gogh

No se puede vivir sin amar.

—Malcom Lowry,
Under the Volcano

Don't I need more authority for what I'm doing?

—Lyndon B. Johnson

—PART ONE—

Chapter One

Tuesday Night, Wednesday Morning

She went to her knees beside him and he could smell the clean fresh scent of her soap, of hair slowly drying in the fading sunlight. Their familiarity stabbed at him.

Hold on, he thought.

She helped him build the fire. The kindling was good today—good and dry. The morning rain had been gentle, brief, the afternoon hot. A beautiful day. An easy day. The forest quietly drifting in a warm fall breeze. They worked together silently. And he thought that perhaps it was just that, the very ease and beauty of the day, which had brought them to this.

Because even peace and beauty could betray you. Not everyone died in firefights.

Not everyone died screaming.

There had been plenty of time to think. Time for her to wander all the old clear trails of her dissatisfaction, of all she missed. Alone. Without the boy, and without him.

He looked at her, the wide blue eyes cast down, the mouth tight, the small thick hands busy breaking branches, stripping twigs.

She's getting old, he thought. The brow furrows easily now.

I'm making her old.

He felt a familiar sudden access of rage and tenderness, fury and tears. He turned away.

I cry so easily these days.

In Nam he'd never cried. He'd held it all together, done what he was supposed to do. It was a matter of survival then, not to show weakness, but he couldn't really say what had changed. Wasn't it still a matter of survival? What was he doing here but finding some way to get on? A different woods, sure, a different partner—but the enemy was still out there. A kind of friendly fire. From somebody who would bag you and take you away from here to somewhere you'd be no damn good at all and maybe dangerous to boot. Take you home.

While there was no home. Unless it was this. As though there could ever be. As though the Nam had ever stopped for him.

He felt his guts contract, a collision of two fears. He was afraid to be alone. Deathly afraid. It skittered inside him like a mad dog.

But he could never, never make it out there.

The fire caught and crackled. From somewhere inside him he heard the whine of incoming mortars.

Nobody was taking him out of here. Not ever. Not even her.

What happened, what did you do, when you could no longer trust the one you needed most, when you could no longer trust your partner?

He fed the flames and did not look at her.

Nine years, she thought. Nine years and still he doesn't smile, he doesn't laugh—and for five of those years I've had a child with him, Lee Jr., smart and blond and strong, and still he won't call him by name. He's just "the boy" to him. His only son. And now I've had to send him away again—my one comfort here—because his father's past is surfacing again, I can feel it, the tightrope walking, the anger and frustration building and the paranoia so bad that even to be gentle with us is a struggle for him and he can hurt you, I know he can. Hurt you bad out here.

And now there's another one coming. Another child. Seven months from now. I had wanted a girl.

What if he knew?

Would he be glad?

I don't think so. He's incapable of that, of gladness.

It would be just another thing for him to fear, one more chance for the world to target him and hurt him while he hides here in the bushes. Another terrible drawing-out.

So he doesn't know.

And I sit building a fire for him. The billionth fire between us. Over and over.

While Lee Jr. plays at his grandmom's house, while something new and—to me—something beautiful and exciting grows inside me. While he stares into the fire, eyes so sad one minute, so blank and empty the next. I told him once that if he killed himself I didn't want to be the one to find him, lying out here like some discarded sack. He understood that. He said he

19

did and I believed him, and he promised. But who else is there?

I will find him. I will be the one. I know it.

Who else is there?

If I leave him, who's left? So many times I've asked that question, and every time the weight is heavier than before. I could spend my life in tears for him, for us, had I not gotten some of him burned into me by now, could I not hold back as he does. But it feels like doom to me, this life. Like fate. Like the punishment for some sin and God help me, I feel like a traitor, like Judas, but I've got to stop it.

He scares me.

Nights when he paces at three or four in the morning, up and back in front of the campfire, up and back, and then stops and listens and I can see the muscles of his back go rigid and I know what he's hearing. It's not the night sounds, the frogs, and crickets. It's not this woods here. You can see the sweat gleaming on him, pouring down his back—and the night might even be a cool one, but it doesn't matter. He's in another forest and it's hotter there. He's listening to his buddies dying, groaning in their sleep. He's hearing shelling, firing. It's more than remembering.

He's there.

He comes back to me and we talk. He sees I'm awake and he tells me. I listen. I can do this for him, what they could never do back there—they could never really speak to one another. Because they were men, I guess, for one thing, and soldiers—but also because you could never know who would be out there in the jungle, moving closer at the sound of your voice, crawling up to kill you. So at three, four in the morning, at daybreak, at dawn, I can do this for him, I can talk.

And what will he do without that?

I'm his friend, his lover, his comrade-at-arms.

And what will he do without that?

I tell myself it can't be helped, I can't go on. I will not bring another child into the world, to waste ourselves out here. But it's more than that.

I can't be this lonely.

Because he's hardly ever here with me. Not really. He's back there somewhere, miles and years ago, in swamps and heat. I swear I never knew the world could be this lonely.

I can't lie to myself. I know what I'm doing. I'm killing him. I am.

He's a big, strong, thirty-nine-year-old man who knows more about survival than most men will ever need or want to know. He could break me in half, it would be easy, he could break most men in half. Yet his life is frail. So very frail I think the wind could blow it away, so tender.

So I know what I am, and what I'll be tomorrow when I leave here. I can feel his eyes on me now like the eyes of a child abandoned in the forest, can feel them already, like the eyes of cats drowned in paper bags, and I could die myself for the hurt I'm giving him, I could die of my own betrayal. It is betrayal.

I love him. I see him clearly. I have to start living again, but I have no illusions, I know who it is that is leaving him to save her own sad, frightened, alone and lonely self.

21

A killer.
The enemy.
Yet another.

Night fell, and the wind came up chilly from the west.
They piled more wood on the fire, large logs now to
get them through longer and longer stretches of time,
to minimize their effort. They rolled cigarettes from
the can of tobacco, drank coffee. The dog, Pavlov,
a three-year-old shepherd with a nick in its left ear,
curled up opposite them and looked from one to the
other. The man pulled off his high leather boots and
moved his feet forward toward the fire. The woman
got up and brought them blankets from the tent. She
handed him one. He draped it over his shoulders.

After a while the man reached behind him for the
ghetto blaster and flipped through a plastic box of
tapes. When the music came through it was softer than
the crackling of the fire.

Born under a bad sign
I been down since I began to crawl
If it wasn't for bad luck
I wouldn't have no luck at all.

The dog shifted restlessly. Its ears ignored the music
and twitched to the sounds of the night. The man
took a pint of bourbon out of his knapsack, uncapped
it, swallowed, and handed the bottle to the woman.
She stared at it a moment then shrugged and took it
from him.

"You know, don't you," she said.

22

He nodded. "I do."

"It'll have to be first thing in the morning."

"I'll get us some breakfast, give you a hand."

He took the pint back from her and drank again.

"You won't try?" she said.

"I did try."

"It was a while ago."

"Not long enough."

The wind shifted east and blew smoke at him. He didn't seem to mind.

They sat there.

"We'll miss you, Alma," he said. She smiled a little because the dog was included. It was like him.

He drank from the bottle. It was careful, even drinking—not heavy.

She watched him lean back through the pale curl of smoke and wriggle his toes, warming them by the fire. She saw his eyes pool up, then he blinked and they were clear again.

He handed her the whiskey.

"Tell the boy for me . . . tell him his daddy just got mean. That the war did that. Tell him he used to do combat—with civilians, with the police, whatever— that he'd go out looking for it, to set things up, in bars, places like that. You know. Tell him that was what I got to be. And that was why I couldn't be with you out there. Explain to him, you know? When he's old enough.

"And if anybody ever tries to draft him, kill them. Kill the son of a bitch for me. I mean it."

He turned the music louder. He tossed the cigarette into the fire and shook his head.

"Fuck me," he said. "Ah, fuck me. Don't tell him nothin'."

She reached a hand across to him. He took it and began to cry.

The dog sat watching them as she slowly drew him toward her and down to the cool hard-packed earth.

It was hours before dawn when she woke. Like an animal alert to danger she was instantly awake. He was gone.

She peered through the flaps of the tent. The fire burned wide and high, almost recklessly this near to her. She saw him on the other side of it, the dog Pavlov following in his footsteps just a few paces behind. It was a scene she was familiar with except for the size of the fire. She turned back inside and slipped on a pair of shoes. She heard him muttering, the dog whining.

She stepped outside into the flush of heat while the breeze played cool across her back. The dog heard her first, turned in her direction and took a few steps toward her, then hesitated between the two of them. As she passed she stroked its muzzle.

"Lee?"

". . . by the carload, straight through Cu Chi . . ." she heard.

She approached slowly.

He faced the stand of elms, black now in the moonless night. She saw the glow of his cigarette, the trailing wisp of smoke. She watched him take two long strides to the left, three to the right. She knew she should not surprise him.

". . . open-housing project was what they called it.

You just fly the hell over and then you drop a couple thousand leaflets tellin' 'em to get out, pick up your stuff and run, then you wait a few minutes and bring in some choppers and bomb the sucker away, level it, level the sonovabitch! 'Doze it, torch it. See some twenty-five *papa-sans* out there after that living in foxholes, fifty, sixty years old. Hell, you gotta live *somewhere*, right? And there *ain't* no *ville* anymore, 'cause we just plowed it under. Village is a memory, man! Village is gone! Bulldoze it right to the bare *ground* . . ."

"Lee . . . ?"

"So they talk to you. Fifty feet away hiding in foxholes out there in the bushes, chattering away . . ."

She touched him on the shoulder.

". . . chattering like birds . . ."

She squeezed the shoulder gently and he stopped and half turned toward her, dropped the cigarette and ground it under his heel.

"What the fuck you want?"

"Are you all right?"

"You care?"

"Oh god, Lee. Of course I care."

He nodded. "Sure. Of course you do."

But the voice was cool, deliberate, and she knew he was not there for her anymore.

"Come get some sleep," she said. "Come inside."

"Can't."

"Come on."

"Where's Sprinkles? Where's that friggin' cherry?"

"He's not here, Lee. Sprinkles isn't here. Come on now."

"Fuck it. Leave me alone."

25

"Come on, Lee."

"I'm supposed to sleep?"

"Yes."

"Really?"

"Yes."

"I'm supposed to sleep now, when, ah . . . when we got all these papa-sans and mama-sans scattered all the hell over the place, livin' in *wheel ruts? You* want me to get some sleep? Unh-unh. No can do. Got work to do. Got cleanup. So screw all that and the horse you rode in on."

"Please, Lee."

"You heard me."

He turned completely toward her and she saw that it was useless. The face had gone pale and hard, the eyes glittered. In the eyes she saw an old familiar look that had grown more and more frequent these past three weeks, that spoke to her of some cold, hard alienation of the soul, a strange blankness that seemed to her like some synaptic misfire, some cerebral heart murmur that would yield to no outside analysis, much less to outside urgings.

It was as though he suddenly wore a mask and not a face at all—no, as though he *were* the mask yet somehow lurked beneath it too. Lee, in league with what possessed him. It was times like these that he frightened her most and made her saddest. Because there was so little hope for a man who could do this, who had to do this just in order to survive.

She walked back to the tent. The dog followed.

And tomorrow it would all be over. She would be gone. For good. After all these years. The thought brought tears to her eyes. But tears did not have the power to make her stay.

Good night, she thought. I love you.

She crept inside. The dog stood watching her a moment, then lay down just outside the tent flaps between her and the fire. She looked at the dog and almost cried again. She pulled the sleeping bag over her and closed her eyes. She realized she hadn't even bothered to take off her shoes. She wouldn't now. It was barely three hours till daybreak.

Once, much later, she heard him opening the tin of tobacco, and then heard his heavy footfalls as he moved away toward the trees. She heard him cry out once—an animal sound, pained and hollow—and then till morning heard him talking, moving, prowling in the dark.

CHAPTER TWO

Wednesday

McCann watched him trudge up the hill along the well-worn path to the shed. He looked to be carrying about a hundred pounds of weight there, the raw dope heavy with morning dew, distributed into four black garbage bags tied together like two pairs of saddlebags and slung over his shoulders. The dog ran out ahead of him, already aware of McCann standing there and eager with the scent of him. Got to wash this jacket, he thought. Gettin' fusty.

He wondered where the woman was. Or the kid.

He calculated quickly. A hundred pounds would be about five plants trimmed of main and secondary shoots, or a third of a plot. Once cured and cleaned you would get about half a pound per plant or two-and-a-half pounds. At fifteen hundred bucks per pound Lee Moravian was bringing roughly $3,700 worth of prime California stuff up the hill to him.

First harvest.

He glanced at the watch straining at his wrist and smiled, the heavy red beard sliding upward and out like an inverted mushroom. The note in his post-office box had said six A.M. and his watch now read

6:03. He knew Lee carried no timepiece. Even for a vet that was pretty damn good again.

He'd want a drink, thought McCann. You worked like a packhorse you deserved one. He walked back into the shed where the lines were already strung, empty, waiting, and took the fifth of Cutty off the floor. Lee would drink anything, smoke anything—but for McCann it was scotch whiskey or nothing, a taste he'd acquired since Nam. He brought it outside.

He was feeling pretty good even without the Cutty—because what you had here was another sweet September morning. Hell, a man could almost stay alive on a day like this. It was nearly October. But you didn't feel the seasons change so much in California. The pot did, somehow, but you didn't. And for a man born and raised in northwest Washington, where it was too damn cold for over half the year, that arrangement was just fine.

He wondered where Moravian was from. He'd never cared to ask him.

They'd met in '67, in basic training at Fort Jackson, South Carolina. Moravian was just a tall, shy, skinny kid then—while McCann already kicked in at 250 pounds. They traveled in different circles there. But then they did their AIT together—Advanced Infantry Training—and there was a little drinking that went on nights, a little after-hours poker, enough so you could get to know and like one another. Then that was it for a while. Because Moravian got sent to West Germany to train with the dogs, while he climbed onto a Continental Airlines jet bound for Saigon, the Republic of South Vietnam. He was assigned to the 25th

Infantry Division, to work the Iron Triangle, War Zone C.

Three months later he's taking an early-morning piss in Cu Chi. He fills up the piss tube, shakes it off and turns around and there's Moravian, a whole lot bigger now and grinning at him, standing in the mist. "I hear you got to watch for leeches in them things," says Moravian. "Not in that one you don't," says McCann. "Not now."

That was what he knew in terms of history. But then he guessed it was enough. Dog Platoon, Moravian was, until he asked for the transfer to front-line infantry. And even that was point. Moravian and his attack dog way the hell out in front of their outfit hunting Cong and booby traps—a six-foot-one, hundred-and-ninety-pound standing, walking target. First to draw fire damn near each and every time. Grenade charges to blow your feet up. Bouncing Bettys to chop up your guts and balls. The man to beat, your basic local gunslinger. Billy the Kid, John Wesley Harding, and the O.K. Corral all rolled into one and humping through the elephant grass. It made his own gig look easy.

His was just a little number called the Tet Offensive— 34,000 dead in ten days. Nothing to it. That and the sweeps through the Triangle as company RTO. Fire ants. Leeches. Bamboo vipers. Malaria.

But he wouldn't have traded it for what Lee went through. Walk point? Hell, no. No way. He'd done it once. It was too damn lonely out there, and too scary.

The Dog Platoon. Good god.

And here was Pavlov, the shepherd, breaking into a

run up the hill to him, tail whipping back and forth like he'd found his mother for god's sake, true love at last. A good animal. Trained to kill or not to kill as the case may be. Moravian had done a job on him. He skidded to a stop in front of McCann and the man bent down into his steamy, doggy breath and ruffled the hair at his collar.

Then he looked up at Moravian and nodded.

"How'd you do?"

"I just took out the early ones. It all looks good, though. Be sixteen feet again, most of them. I'll give the rest one more week, tops, then harvest."

McCann looked at him. He wasn't even breathing hard. And McCann guessed the plots to be easily over a mile and a half away. He thought of his own ballooning bulk and the smokes and the Cutty and was duly impressed.

"So you'll be coming up with what? Fifty plants? A thousand pounds?"

" 'Bout that."

"Hope you got a camel."

"Just me and the dog." He shrugged. "I figure five trips. Six maybe. You can be here, say, a week from Wednesday?"

"I can do that, sure. No problem."

"Good."

He wondered about Lee's wife again. The last few years she'd been up here for the harvest. It was a pretty big job for a man to do alone. But like most of the grunts he knew who were living on the land, Moravian trusted nobody. Not even McCann knew where the plots were laid this year. It was wife and family or nobody at all—and now he guessed it was nobody. He smelled a breakup. He thought of the line from that play: "Ah *smell* mendacity." But he knew better than to ask about it.

"Care for a drink?"

He handed over the Cutty. Lee drank, wiped the neck of the bottle, and handed it back to him.

"Thanks."

"Never too early, right?"

McCann essayed a smile. The guy looks terrible, he thought. Like he sleeps standing up. Maybe on one leg.

He took a long pull from the bottle.

"You hear about Josefsberg yet?"

Moravian looked puzzled.

"You know. Over the mountain here, near Danvers."

"Oh yeah. What about him?"

Figures, thought McCann, that Moravian had forgotten Josefsberg, even though he knew they'd met a couple of times and they had the growing in common. A man got pretty well isolated out here. Your concerns pared down to food, shelter, crop, and water. He knew the feeling. He'd done it himself, once, for about a year's time right after he was evacuated. Got this shit together, did one harvest, figured it out as best he could and then came home. One of the lucky ones, he guessed. Because there was still something left to come home to. Something. The wife had stuck.

But he remembered what it was like. You knew your neighbors by sight so you didn't go and shoot them by mistake like you might just do a trespasser if you were hungry or crazy or desperate enough, and that was about all you needed to know about them. There were damn few sources of news here. And besides, Josefsberg was not a vet. So why should Lee care.

He told him anyway.

"What it is, is that the man got into his carrot patch."

Lee frowned. "All of it?"

"Damn near. They found his safe plot first and then four more after that. He'd only planted six. Burned him out right on the spot. All but just that one. A damn shame. You got to wonder who he'd managed to piss off, you know?"

"How do you figure?"

"Well, hell, they left everybody else alone. Lippman's fine. Farrell's fine. You're fine."

He nodded. "I'm okay."

Sure you are, thought McCann. Wonderful. He *knew* that look. Empty as a department store at three A.M. And for a moment he was disgusted with Moravian's woman even though he barely knew her.

"Sure you are," he said.

"That's too bad," Moravian said. "I hate to hear that. I really do."

"'Course you do. It's your livelihood, right? You relate."

And then he thought, jesus, what was he doing, tippy-toeing around like this? You *relate*. What a stupid fucking thing to say. It was pretty nearly offensive. He could only hope it would just fly by. And evidently it did.

Because Lee said nothing, just reached down and began scratching Pavlov's head, massaging the nicked left ear.

"Well," said McCann, "I guess we could get this stuff inside. Sooner I get it up to dry, sooner we can pick it over."

They hauled the bags into the shed. Already it was hot inside, ripe with the good sharp smell of years of curing marijuana. The shotgun stood propped against the doorjamb.

They ducked one of the drying lines and McCann handed Lee the Cutty again.

"Health," said McCann.

"Health."

They opened the bags and looked it over. As usual Lee's quality was very high. You could smell it, see it in the color and the shape of the buds and leaves. He honestly did look forward to tasting the stuff. It would cure in two weeks' time, sooner if the weather held out hot and dry during the day. You could do it in just a single day in the sun, but you lost a lot of quality that way.

"Looks great," he said. "You can be proud of it for sure, if it's all as good as this."

"It's all as good."

"Terrific. Great."

He handed McCann the bottle.

"I don't suppose you'd want to stick around awhile and hang it with me. We could kill the rest of this whiskey."

"No. I've got work to do," said Moravian.

"Right. Good enough."

They stood and ducked the lines and went outside again. The sun was coming up harsh in McCann's eyes. They'd been sensitive that way ever since the malaria.

Lee whistled for the dog—it was some kind of bird-call he guessed, short and soft and kind of pretty, though McCann didn't know shit about birds, really—and the two of them started down the mountain.

A little ways along Moravian stopped and turned.

"You never asked me," he said, "about Alma and Lee Jr."

"I never did," he said. "How are they?"

Here it comes, he thought.

"Fine. Just fine."

And then Moravian stood there a moment, nodding, looking as though there were something more to say or as though he were all alone out there, maybe, thinking, just him and the dog. And it was no fun, that was sure, whatever it was he was thinking.

"That's good," said McCann.

And it was as if that had released him. He turned and walked away.

McCann stood watching him go slowly down the mountain.

It was none of his business, he guessed. No, hell, he didn't guess, he *knew.* But he wondered, quite seriously and not without a little bit of pain for the poor guy, if he had up and killed the both of them.

CHAPTER THREE

It was night and things were losing their shape and color. The stand of trees had gone white. The mud trail snaked toward him black and narrow through the forest.

He was camped in a blind, his first full night alone.

To his right the trees and brush were laid in thick for one or two klicks back until they dropped off into a brook that curved and ran around behind him, flowing faster there, moving outward and away from him, downhill. Then between the rear of his camp and the brook were more woods, more brush, and to the left a wide heavy patch of brambles. There was only one way anyone was going to approach him that would not make a lot of noise and that was straight ahead along the path.

It was easy to trap that if and when he wanted to.

He was safe here.

In the distance, down the path and off to the right, he could hear the dog snuffling through the bushes. The brook behind him made a light liquid percussion. The campfire popped and crackled.

There was beer and soda cooling in the brook but now he was drinking whiskey.

Not too much, he thought, or you'll get to talking to yourself. And how will that be again.

He turned the fish on the spit—a good-sized bass. The can of peas stood cooking off to one side and next to that was his foil-wrapped baked potato. He poked the potato with a stick. It was nearly ready. The peas were practically boiling so he moved them. A few minutes now.

It was very important to eat.

He drank the whiskey and considered what Mc-Cann had told him—about whatsisname, over on the other side of the mountain. The one whose crop got raided. Maybe it was true that in one way or another he'd managed to get someone angry at him, someone with power. It was possible. They were out there for sure. Maybe he was making too much money in somebody's opinion.

Who could tell? It could just as easily be chance, couldn't it? He remembered a guy he knew back in '68, guy named Mitchell, a helicopter pilot who didn't like to have a door on his gunship because without the door he could fly real low over the rice paddies and pop off rounds at dink civilians. Lee doubted the civilians ever thought anybody was particularly mad at them. It was just their miserable rotten luck to be out there in the fields that day when this guy Mitchell, doorless and potshotting, happened to fly over.

It was a dangerous world, right?

This fish now. Swimming along one minute and hooked and gutted the next. Somebody's dinner.

His.

He tested it with the stainless-steel fork. The skin flaked easily now. He pulled it off the spit and put it on his plate, then speared the potato and put that down beside it. Finally he slipped on the old heavy work glove and grabbed the blackened can of peas, its label burned away, poured out most of the juice and spooned the peas into a neat wet pile next to the potato. He took a pull on the whiskey and then began to eat.

See, Alma? he thought. I eat. After that I'll shit, maybe. Possibly belch. Definitely take a leak. And after that if I'm very lucky maybe I'll sleep. You see? Life goes on.

For everybody but this fish here.

He wondered how she was, she and the boy. They'd be at her mother's house, he guessed. Probably for a week at least. Her mother would want them to stay. Well, that would be good for a while. He had no real use for the mother but she'd make things easy for them now. They'd be safe there.

Away from him they'd be safe.

He speared up a forkful of fish.

It was a funny word, safe.

Safe at the plate. Safe harbor. He thought of condoms. Lockboxes. Thumbing back the safety on an M16. Olly-olly-in-free.

It was a funny word to use on him.

He took a drink.

Safe was something he wasn't. Either personally or, by logical extension, to others.

A plain fact of life now. You just accepted it.

Back in college, way back a hundred thousand years before the war, he'd have thought that a terribly melodramatic way to put things. Heyyyyy! What do you *mean,* safe? Like most kids—the educated types, anyway—he'd been into hairsplitting, equivocation, he'd negotiate an idea to death. The world was relative, wasn't it? Remember Einstein? Things were not black and white. You just couldn't *say* that a man was basically dangerous to others. I mean, what kind of shit was that? Next you'd say darkies gotta dance. Sure there were circumstances in which almost everyone would kill. Of course! Just as there were circumstances in which almost *no* one would kill. It all depended on the, ah, *circumstances.*

D-minus, kid. You've never seen a killer. A good killer. Which is the next best thing to a force of Nature.

You never even dreamed one.

Because what he'd never known back then was that safety was an all-or-nothing proposition. He knew it now. It didn't matter one damn bit to a passenger in some jetliner in a 300-mile-an-hour vertical nosedive wind that flying was, relatively speaking, a nice safe way to travel. What mattered was that he was dying, that this guy was about to die, because this particular plane at this particular time was on its way into a concrete runway. He wasn't *in* any other airplane, any of those good safe steady ones coming and going from Rio to Tahiti and back again, serving cocktails, running movies, making the statistics work.

So that safety—or danger—was personal first and

always. Personal and immediate. Or else it wasn't there at all.

And sure, some men would always kill and some would never, but the important thing was not that or the universe of souls in between but exactly who is sitting next to you at McDonald's today and what is in his suitcase, because if it's dirty socks you're fine and if not, who knows?

He finished the bass. Tossed the head and backbone into the bushes. Scraped his plate.

I am the hurricane, he thought.

And so are they. We together.

Pretty good, he thought, he liked that idea. He saw himself suddenly turning in a wide-screen vortex—a tornado, actually, a twister along with businessmen, generals, agents, cops, a couple of guys from the FBI, crazy old farmers who'd murdered their wives and brothers for land and money and buried them out in the back forty, Wall Street brokers who drank and whipped the kids, Patton, Capone, Nixon, taxmen, porn stars, junkies, nuns, priests, Huns, slopes—all the great wide slaughterhouse-company of creation from Neanderthal to Hitler and beyond riding the storm like Dorothy and Toto in *The Wizard of Oz,* riding this beautiful color fantasy-storm of friendship, belonging, brotherhood, toward the lie that said there just ain't no place like home. Were we betrayed, he thought. Robbed. Were we ever.

I am the hurricane.

That was good. That was right on the money.

He wished he could have said it to Sprinkles. Sprinkles would have liked that.

The dog came trotting down the path, late for dinner. Lee held out his hand and let him smell the fish, gone now but he wasn't very fond of fish anyway, and felt the cold wet nose press against the tips of his fingers. He did that often. It was a chance to make sure the dog was healthy. The dog sniffed and then stepped back a bit, watching him patiently, eyes glittering in the firelight. He reached behind into the knapsack by the tent and took out a can of dog food, rummaged around some more and found the food dish. He used the P-38 on the can and emptied it into the dish. The food smelled strongly of what it was, meat and grains and vitamins. Pavlov seemed to like this shit but it offended him, and he thought that tomorrow they'd do some hunting, get something fresh for him other than the fish.

What he really liked was to watch the shepherd with a bone, a good bone, a big bone—the bigger the better. The brows seemed to furrow in concentration then, the eyes seemed to narrow. There was something wolfish about him then, something genuine and not very doggy at all. It was good to watch him work a bone, smelling it, licking it, sizing it up in a way, then pulling the meat off first, holding it almost delicately between the two front paws and pulling with the nippers and incisors, neck and shoulder muscles working, the dog doing just what he was designed to do, until the scraps that were left were not worth bothering with that way and called for a different strategy. So that then there'd be the sound of gnawing as he scraped it diligently, methodically, using the side teeth mostly, and you were aware of the power of the jaws, the usefulness of all these tools he had. Then finally, much later, late into the night sometimes, the joints would start snapping farther back in his mouth and you knew he was after the marrow.

He liked that. He liked its thoroughness, the sense of purpose and concentration, the lack of waste.

You watched him eat this doggy crap and he was a different animal altogether.

"Tomorrow," he said, "we'll bag an elephant."

The dog looked at him. The big brown eyes expectant for a moment, then losing interest as nothing in particular was forthcoming.

If I died, he wondered, would Pavlov eat me?

The Cong ate dogmeat.

He watched the nose dip down into the nearly empty dish, snuffling for crumbs.

Hell, I wouldn't put it past him.

He remembered how Alma had pleaded with him. *If you kill yourself, Lee,* she said, *don't let me find you.* She'd said that over and over. Begged him. *Don't do it where I'll find you.*

A reasonable request, he thought. Except that it would never have been her anyway. They both should have known that. It would be the dog. It would have to be. The dog would find him.

And have himself some dinner, he thought.

And that, he thought, was the bottom line to everything.

The stars were out. Dipper. North Star. Cassiopeia. He drank some more whiskey and considered once again the raid on whatsisname's. What was it Mc-

Cann had said? *The man got into his carrot patch*. Right. I'd better fortify, he thought. Got an investment here.

He could do a few things. It wouldn't stop the police particularly but it could discourage others, and the cops had to get their information somewhere. Usually from locals. He'd do what he could to discourage them.

"And then we'll go hunting," he told the dog.

It was not quite talking to yourself. He accepted that and continued drinking.

By midnight he was asleep. The bottle was nearly empty.

He dreamed that it was Christmas, and his mother— now thirty-six years dead—had given him all these presents, especially records, dozens and dozens of new LPs which were largely rock 'n' roll and those largely Elvis, but also some jazz and classical, and he'd been playing them in the basement of their house in Maine, the one he grew up in, where they'd always had the Christmas tree when he was a kid—he'd been playing these records happily until some corporate types—four of them, friends of his father's he seemed to think though that could hardly be right— until some corporate types in three-piece suits and hairpieces came down the stairs to commandeer the space and kick him out—so that then he went upstairs to his mother's big bedroom to thank her, to tell her how extravagant it all was and how much he liked the records and especially the Elvis, and she looked at him from where she lay in bed and said, I

43

had to. And he said, Why? And she said, I had to *please* you. And he said Why? again. Because when I don't, she said, you look at me in that way you have. You know. You know the way you have. You look like Charles Manson.

When he woke he was out of the sleeping bag and huddled at the base of a cypress tree with his arms across his knees and the dog lying curled beside him, and the sun was up, and the day was still, there was no wind.

CHAPTER FOUR

Thursday

Kelsey rolled away from her and tried to control his breathing. He felt like panting. But it wouldn't quite do to let her see what a pack and a half a day was doing to him. She saw it anyway.

"I can't believe it," she said. "How you can be this decent in bed and this out of shape at the same time. Listen to you."

"Decent?" he said. *"Decent?"*

"It's true. You're a mess."

"It's all your fault," he said.

"Sure it is."

"It'll have your name on it. The heart attack will." She smacked him open handed on the belly.

"Michelle's bullet."

She laughed. When bodybuilders laughed, he thought, their bodies looked even better. He glanced down at her and watched the stomach muscles define themselves in tiny golden spasms. Beneath his neck her right arm felt hard and soft at the same time. It felt odd to him to lie there on her arm—another kind of role reversal—but in truth her body had more tolerance for his weight than his for hers. And that was just the way it was with them.

He looked at her and it occurred to him again that he probably admired her as much as he desired her. Or thereabouts. To have taken what was naturally yours and perfected it the way she had was something he understood both instinctively and practically. And he felt she had made something beautiful here. A kind of living sculpture, generated in her imagination, in her vision of herself as perhaps she might be, long before it had come to fruition. Then to deliver the goods had been rigorous, painful, tedious, and thoroughly self-absorbing—and continued to be. In that sense she was as far beyond the general run of models who were born with beauty but were not engaged in shaping it beyond adherence to the usual professional rigors of sleep, exercise, diet, and the appointments with cosmeticians and stylists as he was from the hack who wrote slick TV ad copy for a living. Even the narcissism of it was familiar. If you wrote novels, good novels, you did it sweating in a mirror.

So that now to look at her and appreciate her was to pay tribute to the mind that made her as well.

He granted that the raw material was high quality. The proportions of leg to thigh, thigh to hip, hip to torso would have delighted a Leonardo. The head was strongly shaped, with a slightly gamin cast to the chin, which lent a certain delicacy. The eyes were dark, wide—a good, almost Mediterranean contrast to the essential blonde Swedishness of her—the lips full but not heavy, and if the nose was just a touch too long it was still admirably aquiline and she was, after all, a model, and the world still liked a hint of aristocracy there. No, all these things were fine.

But what made you want to look and touch again and again was the interplay between what was natural and what was simply *not given*. The satin-smooth tanned and golden skin, yes, but also the drumhead tightness of it over her back or shoulder or thigh. The deep, soft breasts but also the wide expansive rib cage they rode on and the muscles which drew them high. These things she had made. And it was thrilling to be able to touch them. To be inside her, he thought, was to find the warm liquid softness at the heart of her power—a generative yielding and a fist, both together.

He was a lucky man. The world knew it and he knew it. And if he did in fact admire her as much as he desired her, so far his admiration was unbounded.

The only problem, if you could call it a problem, was in keeping the hell up with her. A woman nineteen years younger and undoubtedly capable of wrestling him to the ground.

Though he too could slap a tummy. He did so.

Not a quiver. Amazing.

He stroked her there.

"What do you want from me? I'm an old man. I've got habits. Years and years of habits."

"Yes, and I'm telling you they're going to kill you. Besides, you're all of forty-three. Big deal."

"You'll kill me."

"Hell, I'm what keeps you fit. Your only exercise."

"Like jogging?"

"Joggers get bad feet. I'm better than that."

"How much better?"

"Better."

He rolled toward her and kissed her neck at the collarbone, pleased to find it still damp at the hollow. He loved the smell of her. She smelled vaguely floral, herbal or something, without any sweetness to it. Like cut grass.

"I wouldn't mind," he said.

"What?"

"A really massive coronary. Dying on top of you. Or under you. In the saddle so to speak."

"I would. Jesus! Thanks a lot. Your conversation gets very weird sometimes."

"It could happen. You get to a certain age, it's possible."

"You want to quit? Keep this platonic?"

"I'd more or less rather die first."

"Now you're just trying to charm me."

"You know what George Eliot said, don't you?"

"Not this time. No."

"The fear of poison is feeble against the sense of thirst."

"She said that?"

"Yes."

"Really?"

"Yes."

"You thirsty?"

"Give me, say, twenty minutes."

"Ten."

"Make it twenty-five."

And that was when they heard the car pull in.

Kelsey got up off the bed and went to the window. He saw the tan Mercedes glide around the wide, newly paved circular driveway and stop beside the Jeep parked directly in front of the house. He watched his wife get out of the car, take a box off the passenger seat and walk over to the Jeep, throw its rear doors open and deposit the box inside. Beer, liquor, or soda, he thought, or some of each. She didn't have to do that. He'd told her he'd pick some up tonight or tomorrow morning. But as usual she was more organized than he was.

He turned to Michelle.

"Caroline," he said.

She stretched and sat up in bed and he saw her looking for her robe. It was on the floor beside him. He picked it up and handed it to her.

"You win," she said. "Twenty-five minutes."

He smiled. "Maybe just a little longer than that now."

She belted the robe and stepped off the bed, and you could see in the movement where the twenty years of dancing went.

"Piker."

"I'll make it up to you."

"Damn right you will. Where are my clothes?"

"Other side of the bed."

He slipped on his own robe now.

"Come here," he said.

"Why? You're no good to me anymore."

"Just come on."

She went to him, pulling on her jeans as she did so, the jeans so tight she had to hop a little in order to get them on over her hips, and she was still trying to zip them, her arms making the robe blouse open so that he saw the pale nipples erect again as he took

49

her face in his hands and kissed her. Then she finished zipping and her arms went around him as she returned the kiss.

They heard the front door open. Crisp paper shopping bags being placed on the kitchen counter. It was Thursday and Mary the maid and sometimes cook was off today. Hence the afternoon tryst here. A free day, and a little privacy. It was odd, he thought, how you tended to defer to the inevitable disapproval of people you paid to hang around and wait on you.

"Mmmm," she said, breaking the kiss, "you taste like me."

He laughed. "I'm not surprised."

She pulled away a little. "I want to go see Caroline for a minute. Is that okay?"

"Sure it's okay."

"Yes? Then let me finish dressing, all right? You sure you don't mind?"

"No."

"You can go brush your teeth."

"No, I'll leave you there for a while. I'm going to play with these galleys a little. Free things up for tomorrow. You go ahead. What time's your agent meeting you, anyway?"

"Six thirty."

"Okay."

He watched her slip into the blouse and tuck it in, her gestures with regard to clothing always very precise. She sat on the bed to put on her shoes, crossing first one leg and then the other. Even when a woman was your lover, he thought, the voyeur in you did not die. Maybe even expanded a bit.

He sat down at the desk and opened the galleys. Michelle smiled at him. He watched her leave the room.

One of the very few fights he'd had with his wife in eighteen years of marriage was over this desk. And it had lasted weeks. Caroline just couldn't see having the thing in the bedroom. She pointed out that they each had their own study. She pointed out that this was Bel Air, not the apartment in New York City. They would be giving parties, entertaining her clients. The bohemian was not appreciated. But it was often Kelsey's habit to get up in the middle of the night to jot down a half-formed idea or some fragment of a dream, or to do some work just before bed at night, and this was a luxury he'd promised himself once he became successful, and he was damned if her sense of decor, excellent though it was, or California's judgments about movie-colony chic, were going to wrest it from him. So in the end he got the desk, with one compromise: There would be no typewriter. That was all right. It had never been essential to the idea in the first place. Caroline didn't know that, and that was okay too. In a fight everyone had to win something.

The galleys were fine, really. Just a reprint of a short novella he'd written years ago, part of a new anthology, sent to him as a courtesy from the publisher. All he'd found to correct thus far was a single misplaced comma. They all should be that good, he thought.

He heard them talking outside in the kitchen. Thank god they could talk to one another.

He remembered what it had been like with Eva— Evita Peron he'd called her, though she was German.

51

Caroline of course was already used to him by then, so she had been her usual civilized self. Loving, attentive, cultured, and totally unflappable. But merely to mention his wife to Eva was enough to coax sparks out of her eyes and stiffen every hair on her curly red head. It was amazing to him that a woman who had danced the lead little girl in *The Nutcracker* at age ten had grown up the possessor of so foul a mouth and so essentially graceless a disposition. The sex had been good—excellent, to be honest—but with something always burning on the stove like that it could never have lasted.

He wondered what they were talking about.

She'd left the door open.

He got up and opened it further. They had good isolation up here at the end of the drive so that outside it was very quiet, very still. If he sat on the edge of the bed and listened he could hear them pretty well.

It was a nice clean mix of tones. Both were handsome voices. His wife's deeper, drowsier, the Massachusetts accent still there—imparting that delightful bogus Britishness that the literary and film worlds in general and her own more important clients in particular seemed to love. ("She sounds so *influential*," Evan Hunter had told him once. "It's like having Henry Kissinger out there gunning for you.") Michelle's higher and lighter, a sleek young California sound that spoke of money and sun, easy composure, power, health, and rock 'n' roll.

Ah, he thought, they've gotten down to it.

". . . I wouldn't say it *was* if it wasn't," Caroline was saying. "I wouldn't. Honestly. If I felt it was going to be difficult in any way whatsoever I'd simply stay home tomorrow. I mean, I'm getting sort of old to go traipsing around in the woods as it is, don't you think? So if I weren't pretty certain about it . . . well, why bother? Really, Mich, don't worry at all."

"I know. Sure. I just really wanted to . . ."

He heard the refrigerator door close, then the water running in the sink, and then Caroline's voice again.

". . . and my only *real* reservation is why Bernie insists on inviting that damned Charles Ross along."

"I know what you mean. I can't figure it either. I think maybe Bernie feels sorry for him or something."

"Believe me, no one need feel sorry for Mr. Charles Martin Ross."

And then there was more water running, and he heard someone rummaging through the pots and pans, looking for something. Then he heard them laughing. Good, he thought.

I can't believe it. They're actually getting along. *Still.* He felt like a man who had done something wonderful without knowing what in hell it was and now somebody was giving him the key to New York City. Have mercy on this poor sinner. Keep it going.

There wasn't much left he wanted in life. One more book that he could feel was really fine, maybe. Definitely that. Absolutely. He needed that badly. But he wasn't greedy. One would do. So that he could retire from it all if he wanted to with some sort of honest respectability, at some sort of peak. He knew it would get him remembered. Naturally he wanted that.

And once he'd wanted children. That was no longer necessary. He was pretty much content now to attempt to live with whatever grace and dignity he could muster as the last of his line—if he could manage that much.

Money he had. Turned out it meant both less and more than he'd thought it would. But he was in very little danger of going broke again.

No, there was only one other thing that he wanted with any kind of seriousness at all, and that was to hold on to both these women.

He was aware of it as a kind of hubris, a kind of egomania. He knew it was not the sort of wish that was likely to be granted. But what each one gave him was so necessary now—so much and so different, the one from the other—that the thought of losing either one of them was enough to make him privately crazy, sleepless, terrified, and the thought of having to choose between them unthinkable.

He hadn't shown them how deep it was running in him these days. He couldn't—he was afraid it would spook them. And he wouldn't now. It was enough that they were getting along, at least for the moment. Perhaps you could build a real affection on that, something that would last awhile.

It did not occur to him to wonder why a forty-three-year-old successful, even famous, writer should care so much or try to manage something so quixotic. He knew the answer to that one.

". . . I've got a pair of hiking boots that should fit you," Michelle was saying.

Good, he thought. Take the boots. Share things. Hang in there.

He went back to the desk he had fought very doggedly for, over ten years ago, and shuffled through the galleys of his old novella, looking for misplaced commas.

CHAPTER FIVE

The trap was called the Malayan Swing.

Back in Nam you'd have used bamboo—but here it was saplings, lashed together with twine, pulled back off the trail and camouflaged so that when you hit the trip wire this thing came at you out of nowhere, a four-by-four wooden grid that hit you in the face and chest like a flyswatter, and hit you hard.

It could rearrange your teeth some or knock you unconscious.

To an intruder it was very annoying.

Still he thought about the police and wondered if he should make it the old way.

The old way was lethal.

They'd learned it from the VC. The VC would add short pointed stakes to the gridwork, so that when it came at you it was like walking into an iron maiden— except that here she was moving down at thirty miles per hour if you got the tension right.

It was normally enough to kill the point man on contact and scare the rest sufficiently so that they dove for cover. So then they'd planted more stakes—dozens of them, in double rows—all along both sides of the trail. They'd smeared them with buffalo shit to decay and ferment and they were honed down nice and sharp. You went for cover headfirst if you were scared enough, you often did, and he remembered peeling guys off them leaving bits of eyes and brain behind.

He pulled the twine tight and finished the grid.

You could take out a squad of cops with the Swing and *pungi* stakes and no one would ever find them. One man could. Just walk around behind them once it was over and finish whatever was left alive and screaming.

Then it was just cleanup.

There were advantages to doing it that way and he tried to consider them coldly. But in the end it was too much. A kind of overload. He could feel the notion of active warfare again burning, crackling like a downed high-tension wire in the back of his brain. It had been years since he'd killed a man—years even since he'd carried a gun. Alma had pointed out that too often if he had one he tended to use it. On bad nights he'd fire at shadows sometimes. Crazy as hell. And it was bad with a kid around. Now there was just this fancy British-made high-tech crossbow, and that was different somehow.

No, he was not going to start that again. Not unless he had to. Bad enough to have to live like this, as though entering an enemy zone all the time—or more accurately, trying to skirt one. There was nothing he could do about that. But take it one step further and you were in really deep shit this time, fighting for your life. It was not a fight you would win. This was

America, after all, The World. You could not just frag
your company CO for giving you an order that might
kill you and expect to walk away from it. All he had
to do was start killing cops and the cops would not
stop coming. He had already lost one war. He knew
how it felt.

This would do. It would help buy him time to complete the harvest. The other he would not think about.
Could not.

Not unless he had to.

He strung it back and laid the trip wire. By the time
he was done his face was dripping wet and his pants
were soaked halfway to the knee with sweat. The dog
sat quietly dozing all the while. Dogs, he thought; dogs
were the picture of innocence. The VC knew the
grunts were all suckers for them so in Pleiku they'd
sew satchel charges into a dog's belly and then when
you went to pet him they would blow it on you.

He sat back on the ground and checked the wire,
its lead to the swing. You wouldn't know it was there
unless you'd built it. Three of the plots lay off this
trail, the rest off another one a little less than a mile
away. He'd rig a second trap over there and then he
and the dog could do some hunting.

Busy day, he thought. Good to keep busy. Good to
forget that now he was all alone out there.

He had forgotten for a while.

He slid the knife, hatchet, and machete into his
equipment belt and retrieved the crossbow from
where he'd hidden it nearby in the brush.

"Come on," he said to the dog.

His first words of the morning.

By roughly two o'clock the second trap was finished.

He ate some lunch and then hiked the mile and a half to the campground, which was deserted, went down over the hill to the pond, and shucked off his clothes.

The water was cold, felt good after the heavy, sweaty work. His body felt lighter now, as though the water had the power to counter the humbling effects of gravity on his muscles. He was a good swimmer. Always had been. There was a place in Maine where they used to go as kids and it was much like this. Called Little River. You'd hike past some gravel pits and then into the woods, and you could go naked there. That was a big deal then, when you were say nine or ten or eleven. Go out to Little River and play Nature Boy, Nature Girl. There was a tire on a rope they'd hung from a tree out over the water there and you could swing on it and drop down. Naked. Girls with breasts barely budding. Boys hairless and lithe as snakes.

Then his father had gotten wind of it somehow and walloped the hell out of both his sister and him and that was the end of that. Told the other kids' parents too, he remembered. Said it was his duty.

Well sure it was.

As far as Lee was concerned his father was nobody's nightmare exactly but a bad piece of business all the same. World War II antiaircraft gunner, gung ho as hell, your basic '40s enlisted man. A logger and then a foreman for thirty-five years after that and a total raw-meat specimen of barely literate asshole.

His mother had died of the flu before he knew

her. He vaguely remembered her making half-burned ginger cookies for some bake sale or something and then he remembered her dying.

Funny that he'd dreamed about her. He did now and then. This gray little lady with the pale, sad, indistinct face. Like the ghost of somebody.

He had no idea where his sister was. The last he'd heard she'd joined a commune run by some twelve-year-old maharishi guru yogi. A long way from the swimming hole.

They were all a bunch of goddamn joiners.

But he did have big hands, though, my father.

He swam to the shoreline and lay there awhile, half in the water and half in sunlight. The dog was off roaming somewhere.

If the water were a little warmer, he thought, I could easily fall asleep here.

He lay back and let the water have him.

And he was not surprised particularly when the images started coming, fast on the image of his father. They were pulling guys out of tunnels and spider holes. Cong, not Sprinkles this time, thank god, not that stupid cherry, but skinny little guys naked to the waist, dragged by a piece of twine looped under one armpit and over the neck because you didn't want to touch them, hauled out of the dirt by some meatless shred of arm, old emaciated corpses, legless, headless. Long dead.

He shook himself, blinked. Pulled himself out of the water.

He saw movement to the left of him, just behind a

clump of brush there. He shook his head again, ignored it.

He reached for the canvas knapsack, bunched it up
to his nose and mouth and breathed into it, trying to
control the hyperventilation. He closed his eyes but the
Cong came back again, just this one alive and bleeding
through a dirt-encrusted eye patch, and he knew what
the eye looked like under there, gangrenous blue meat,
so he opened his own eyes again. One. Two. Three.

In a moment he had it under control.

Okay, good, he thought. You got it.

He was sweating.

He whistled for the dog.

He put on his shirt and pants and by that time the
dog had appeared, excited and ready to go because
he knew what the crossbow meant, he'd been waiting all day, and it was getting on to that time when
they either did or they didn't.

He knew what the dog's vote was.

Gimme a minute, he thought.

He strapped the equipment belt on and straightened the axe handle.

He took a breath.

Experimentally he closed his eyes again. Then
opened them.

Sometimes they stayed, sometimes they walked
right out into the daylight with him but not this time,
it was okay.

He picked up the crossbow and motioned to the
dog. They walked up the hill through the camp-
grounds and deep into the forest.

CHAPTER SIX

Michelle tugged lightly at the steering wheel, edging the Mercedes down off Bellagio and slowly around the corner. The car's power was essentially useless now, checked by the hairpin meanderings of a steep mountain road, by noise regulations, by a strictly enforced 30-mile-an-hour speed limit, and by plain tradition—because while it well may be that you did not Go Gentle into That Good Night, you damn sure did go gentle in Bel Air.

There was nothing in her that would bridle at the fact: she was all for curbs on power. It was a natural thing, really, and something you learned working out—ideally, force should be met by another force as exactly its equal as possible. Not more and not less. There, in one direction or the other, lay injury. The pulled muscle, the torn tendon.

Bel Air was a kind of force, so you met it appropriately.

In her work she had only recently attained that kind of equilibrium. The days of tatami mats and lofts in downtown Manhattan—six girls to a loft—of go-sees and rejections and showcasing for next to nothing just to be seen in the fashion magazines were, thank god, over. A year ago she could barely get through the crowded agency switchboard to talk to her booker. Today she had the woman's private number. Elaine's as well. And that in itself was power.

Since the Calvin Klein contract there had been no more go-sees, only requests to shoot product categories other than perfume, and she chose them carefully. Made sure they were positioned correctly for her. Her book included work from Donna Karan, Anne Klein, Norma Kamali, Giorgio Armani, Emmanuelle Khanh, Karl Lagerfeld—all the sort of people who designed for curves and strength and health. Scavullo, Gilles Bensimon, Avedon, Annie Leibovitz, and plenty of others all understood what special qualities she was selling and liked to photograph her. Even Helmut Newton had shot her poolside, dripping wet, standing perfect bodied, powerful, and wild-eyed over a drowned, handsome swimmer, dead for love of her.

Her clarity in these matters had made her rich. With the $250,000 from Calvin and the other jobs, she stood to make over $500,000 this year and probably a million the next. So that she was finally on something of an equal footing with the fashion power brokers, since she would not for much longer be dependent upon them. Her "fuck you" money was almost there. She knew the opportunity to move into areas other than fashion would not be far behind. Readers of *Cosmo, Elle, Vogue,* and *Glamour* were used to seeing her face on the cover; now the readers of *People* would get used to her too. Her face had a name now, it was this year's face, this year's look, and it felt quite good and natural to her.

This will pass, she thought. Models lasted longer these days but not forever. But she was willing to let it pass. In fact she looked forward to it. By then there would be something else, some other, newer force to challenge her. Perhaps Hollywood. It would be interesting, she thought, to head a major entertainment complex, to produce and package films.

It would also be nice to have a child.

Maybe Kelsey's child.

And she wondered how Caroline would feel about that. How she'd feel even a couple of weeks from now.

It was hard to know with any certainty. Caroline, she was learning, was quite a woman.

She turned onto Stone Canyon Road. The wind and the hiss of her tires on the tarmac were the only sounds. Almost there, she thought, and not another car on the road the entire time. Even if you could ignore the luxury of the homes and the sculpted grounds, the isolation alone would tell you there was incredible money here. The extent of it amazed her every time. For the rest of the world Kelsey, Caroline, and Michelle were all individually rich. Very rich. Here they were still poor relations. Below, on Sunset Drive, it was rush hour. Cars pressed bumper to bumper, bellowing smog. Bel Air, however, knew no such thing as rush hour. It resisted the press of the growing, sprawling city beneath it the way gravity resisted the urge to fly. Sure, you could get on a plane and fly on through now and then, there was nothing stopping you, but you lingered where you did not belong at considerable risk of crashing—and crashing hard—what fueled the jets of these particular hills being among the most expensive substances imaginable.

She pulled into the parking lot of the Hotel Bel Air and handed her keys to the attendant. He held the door for her, smiling. "Evening, Miss Ryan." She nodded and returned the smile. She walked through the covered arcade past stands of orange tree, lemon tree, banana, bamboo, and palm. She crossed the wide, stone bridge that arched above the swan pond, saw two of the birds gliding there, one preening and one upended, searching for something in the water. The garden was a riot of bright flowers.

She turned at the reception area and walked up the steps to the piano bar. She smiled at the barman. His name had escaped her again but it was the big man, the marine, the one who'd served in Vietnam. Kelsey would know.

"Your party's over there, I believe," he said, discreet about not using her name. There were eight or ten people at the bar and some had already noticed her. She looked around the corner into the second, larger room where the piano was. And there was Elaine, sitting in an armchair, sipping a glass of wine. Hiding.

"Thanks," she said. She walked to the table.

The Chanel print was lovely but Elaine looked drawn and tired. It was hard to remember sometimes that the woman had once been quite a beauty in her own right. Michelle had seen pictures, though. She would bet that in the '40s there were men who would have died or killed for her. Now of course there were sixteen-year-old girls who would. But her beauty had grown brittle over the years. She was head of one of the top four agencies in the country, she'd come up hard and fast, and now even the smile had the look of a contract.

They shook hands and Michelle sat down across from her.

"You look lovely," she said.

Elaine waved in dismissal. "I look like hell," she said. "But I just got Margot out from under Casablancas so I really don't give a damn. I bet I look better than he does. The dress is pretty, though, don't you think?"

"Yes. Congratulations."

"Thanks. The little bitch doesn't deserve me."

Michelle laughed. "The way you work, nobody does."

"You do," said Elaine, "or at least you did. I asked you to come to New York, remember? You know I can't stand flying."

"I'm sorry. It's just that Kelsey has this weekend planned. And I really could use the days off. I'm closing on the house in Arizona on Tuesday. And then on Wednesday there's Jamaica."

Elaine lit a Virginia Slim. "I know," she said, "and I still can't see why you're bothering. There's no money in it, for god's sake."

"It's British *Vogue*, Elaine, and I need the exposure in Britain. Plus her designs are really spectacular this year. *Nobody* could wear those swimsuits better than me. So nobody's going to. Plus it's Jim's shoot and he'll make me look terrific. Plus it's *Stephanie of Monaco*. Even you liked that angle."

"I know, I know. I just thought we were through with swimsuits and token money, that's all."

Michelle shrugged. "Somebody designs something I look good in, I want to wear it. I'll give you this much, though—that'll be it for swimwear. At least for this year. Top of the line and that's that. Okay?"

Their waiter appeared. A dapper little middle-aged man in a white jacket. Michelle ordered an Amstel. The waiter nodded and headed for the bar. The lounge was beginning to fill now. About half the tables in their area were occupied. Elaine was looking at her.

"Beer," she said. "You and your beer."

"I like beer."

"You could at least order a Lite or something, for god's sake. It makes me look bad."

Michelle smiled, shook her head. "Michelle's law," she said.

"Huh?"

"The law of compensation. Eat what you like, drink what you like—without reason, naturally. Then work like hell to make up for it. No NutraSweet, no Diet Pepsi. Real sugar and real beer. Potatoes and buttered bread. Then earn the right to do it again the next time."

Elaine sighed. "I'd get very, very fat."

"Not you. You'd whip me in wind sprints in six months' time."

The beer came. The waiter poured it for her. Elaine seemed to study her as she drank.

"How was Paris?" she asked.

"Rained. It never stopped raining. It was fun doing

runway work again, though. Especially with Paulina. We had a good time."

"I saw the designs. It looked like a super collection."

"It was. At least we thought so. Some very nice jersey. The usual great, spectacular pirouettes in fur and leather. Pretty well vintage Claude Montana, I'd say. It should do well."

"It's already doing well," said Elaine.

They sipped their drinks.

They gazed around the lounge.

The piano player sat down at the piano.

"Okay," said Elaine. "Time we cut the bullshit."

Michelle looked at her. "Okay."

She watched Elaine lean forward and press the palms of her hands flat to the table. She knew the gesture. Behind her the piano player adjusted his tails over the piano bench.

"So?"

"What do you want to know, Elaine?"

"What do I want to know? I *need* to know *what in the hell is going on!*"

Michelle sighed. She ought to have expected this would not be easy. "Elaine," she said, "I tried to make you understand on the phone that this trip wasn't necessary"

"Oh good. Not necessary. Jesus Christ! You're pregnant, aren't you?"

"Yes."

"Yes. And it's Bernard Kelsey's kid, right?"

"Of course it is."

"Of course it is. You ass."

"What?"

"I said you ass."

"Elaine."

"You goddamn idiot."

"That's enough, Elaine."

"How could you be so *stupid*."

"I said *enough,* all right? People get pregnant. It happens. I don't need a lecture."

One look at the woman's face and she knew she'd get one anyway. That was okay. She was ready. She watched Elaine draw back, lips tight and cheeks reddening, then lean suddenly forward, striking like a snake. Hell, she *was* half snake. Go on, she thought. She was damned if she'd be shamed by this.

"Don't you give me any of that 'it happens' crap, missy, because you're in *trouble* here—Kelsey is no fucking Billy Joel, you know. He's a goddamn married man twenty years older than you, and the press has been very nice to you so far, *very* nice, a little snigger here and there and some aren't-they-terribly-naughty columns, but nobody has bothered to mention that you've been screwing the guy under his wife's nose, for god's sake, half the time in the same house with her, his wife who is not exactly unknown to the press either, I might add. Just how do you think it's going to set with all those sweet little suburban girls and their equally suburban mothers—not to mention those little yuppie shits in their twenties who figure screwing is synonymous with AIDS or herpes in the first place, who would simply roll over and *die* to think that crazy idiot crap you're doing here, and who just happen to make up half the market for that superfit healthy All-American body, the body you are selling, dear, at least this week—how do you think it's going to sit if we get a baby in the picture? A baby made *a trois* with god knows what humping and fucking and sucking going on between the three of you? Oh I know Caroline has nothing to do with this but the popular imagination staggers! It *loves* to stagger! I warn you. You are not out of the woods yet, Mich. You *need* fashion and you are going to need it for a few years yet to come. And you are *ruined,* baby, if this gets out, you are through. I *promise you!*"

She sat back in the armchair. End of lecture.

Not bad, thought Michelle. She can still play all the strings. And dammit! She's classic, but she's got me all wired and tight and nervous again.

The piano was into a jazzy "Skylark" and Michelle just sat there a moment, letting the tension drain away. Elaine was overreacting but what had she expected? Of course she'd be worried. They'd been together for three years now. And there was truth in what she said.

She ordered another round. Elaine, whose limit was usually one, didn't stop her.

"I promise you, Elaine, it's not going to get out. I won't let it. You want the whole speech? Okay. I know this is no time to have a baby. For lots of reasons. I tried to tell you that on the phone. You didn't have to come here. I have no intention of keeping it. I'm not going to try."

"Fine. So who's performing the abortion? Some intern at L.A. County General? You having it on the lawn? Just how the hell do you expect to keep this *quiet* out here, for god's sake? Who can you trust? I know what I'm talking about, dammit. I know this town. They die and take their telephones to hell with them out here. You should come back with me to the City, go to Larson. He knows you and he'll keep his damn mouth shut."

"It's taken care of. My appointment's a week from tomorrow."

"With who?"

"A doctor."

"Right. A doctor." She nodded.

"Yes. A doctor who'll be discreet. So please, don't worry. I'm only six weeks gone. It's quite simple."

"Who, goddammit!"

"Elaine . . ."

"Who! I've got a right to know who! There's something riding on this from my side too, you know. Plenty riding on it! Jesus Christ, Mich, be fair, will you?"

She took a breath and thought about it. Elaine was right. They were in business together. Telling her was only fair. She supposed it was only hard to say right now because she didn't really know exactly how she felt about this part either. How could she? By anybody's standards it was a little weird.

"His name is Geis," she said. But of course Elaine made no sign of recognition, of course a name was not enough.

"Caroline's doctor."

She watched the agent sit back slowly in her armchair, watched it dawn on her. The piano player was finishing "Skylark" to scattered applause. The waiter brought them their second round. And still Elaine's mouth hung open slightly, struck by the unthinkable.

"Caroline's . . . *Caroline's* doctor?"

"That's right."

She guessed that she might as well tell all of it now. It didn't make much difference and Elaine wanted to know.

She placed her hands flat on the table. Elaine's gesture.

"Caroline's taking me," she said.

CHAPTER SEVEN

Rabbits were tricky but he'd gotten good at them, it was a matter of keying in to the animal once the dog had flushed it and knowing where the jump would come and how far based on size and weight and speed, a fast intuitive computation, and then avoiding that, wanting it on the ground, running, counting on the dog to keep it out in the open, then leading through the crosshairs scope and squeezing off the bolt. Rabbits were plentiful this season. Three sightings in a little less than an hour and he had two of them, one fat female and a smaller male.

The light was fading. The dog trotted briskly at his side. The dog's eyes darted to the ruck on his back where the animals lay wrapped in butcher's paper, slack and still warm as they headed through the brush.

The advantage to the crossbow here was that the kill was nearly silent. A dog and a rabbit running hard for a while and that was about it. You didn't scare away everything for miles. The bow was heavy-gauge aluminum, laminated in plastic. It carried seventy-five pounds of tension, good for sixty feet minimum at seventy-five miles per hour. It had the crosshairs scope, a safety, and a comfortable pistol grip. It was durable and very accurate. The arrows were sharp aluminum bolts, feathered in blues and reds bright and unnatural as a punker's hairdo so you could find them in the brush. Six of them rode in the quiver attached to the stock's base for fast reloading. At close range, a very good weapon indeed.

They walked through the clearing into the forest, getting cooler now, and he could hear the fast-running brook in the distance where the camp was. Instinct and memory made him slow down. The sound of the stream was very distinct, though much fainter than at the campsite, and very familiar. He listened. Just about two klicks, he thought, the same then as now, and he'd listened to the brook all night in the dark, the sound of faraway running water like his life running out from under him while the squad of drinks walked 'round from man to man, all of his guys wounded by then as far as he could tell, and you'd hear some dumb grunt begging them not to shoot, don't shoot, somebody who didn't even sound like himself anymore, Doc or Scag or Wilson though not Sprinkles, not Sprinkles— and maybe it was the warm dead weight on his back that reminded him too. Maybe that was it.

Fuck it, he thought. The dog was impatient and this was a whole other time entirely.

The camp was as he left it.

He put the ruck down by his tent and removed the rabbits. He poured some water in a basin. The dog watched him, tongue lolling, pacing excitedly.

"Down," he said.

The dog sat. He unwrapped the rabbits and walked

to the makeshift drying rack, sat on a rock and opened his pocket-knife. He set the male aside and pinched together the loose skin on the female's back, slit it with his knife, inserted his fingers and tore the skin through from back to belly. He peeled off the lower half like a glove, cut away the tail and the hind feet and pulled the skin completely off the animal. He turned it and peeled the other half the same way, cutting off the head and forelegs. He opened the thin underlayer of skin just beneath the rib cage and flipped out the entrails, then cut away the gland between each of the legs and the body. He washed the carcass and pinned the female to the rack, picked up the male and repeated the process. Then he went through the entrails for the hearts and livers. In under five minutes he was finished.

He built a fire. He cut himself a spit out of green white oak and spitted the carcasses, then cut two crotched uprights and set them into the ground on either side of the fire. When it was hot enough he thrust the rabbits into the flames to sear the meat. Then he put them aside, put some fat in a pan and cooked the hearts and livers for the dogs. He opened a can of potatoes and another can of lima beans. When the fire burned down to coals he placed the spit across the uprights and began to cook the meat, slowly and evenly, and set the two cans on the soft dim outer coals.

He watched the rabbits, the thin pale skin as it darkened, licked with waves of heat. He could smell them.

Napalm was a jelly that would cling to flesh and burn until it burned itself out, there was nothing you could do to put it out until it was ready.

Rabbit, he thought, death's easy.

He got up and walked to the tent, pulled the poncho liner off his stash and picked up a bottle of rye.

He squatted by the fire, turned the rabbit on the spit and drank from the bottle. The whiskey had a rough, sweet edge to it that sickened him at first, then warmed him inside. There was the momentary impulse to forget about eating and finish the rye instead, to give both rabbits to the dog instead of only the smaller male. The dog would like that and maybe so would he for a little while. But he guessed it was important not to let yourself go, to get up at a decent hour and do what you had to do, to shave and take care of yourself and put on clean clothes if you had them. Otherwise you got like Sprinkles and you just didn't care anymore.

He thought about Sprinkles not caring and what happened to them all that made so much difference and he started to cry, two thin tears at first but then a series of deep, racking sobs that were uncontrollable despite him saying, shit, you're slobbering again you asshole, and that stopped only when the dog started whimpering, too, pacing nervously on the other side of the fire, wanting to go to him but unsure of his reception. And it was knowing he was putting the dog through this that stopped him.

He was thinking of Sprinkles often these days. Sprinkles, whose name was given to him by the grunts in Alpha Company because one of the things he'd brought from home and carried in his ruck was a plastic ziplock bagful of chocolate jimmies from his father's candy store, figuring that even if they did have ice cream in Nam they wouldn't have sprinkles, and he used them once in Saigon on the second night they knew each other and once in Pleiku and then spent nearly the rest of his tour waiting to use them again. The goddamn twink. The cherry. He was one of those guys who never seemed to stop being a cherry. Like there wasn't a war there.

Normally you went through stages. Innocence and awkwardness and fear, that was one stage, the first stage. Then you saw a couple of firefights and it was just fear for a while because the innocence went fast with an M16 in your hands—but you did what you were supposed to do more or less and that got you to the next stage, to being pretty good at what you did, whatever you did, and a lot of guys stopped fearing then, got hard or reckless or both. That lasted awhile. Until you got short. Until there was only a month or two left in your tour and then only weeks and then only days, and it was then that you got scared again, because you'd lived this long and you knew you couldn't ever be this lucky, you were going to die—today, tomorrow, the next day—and you were going to die bathed in irony, short as hell, with only the luck you knew you had all along in the end, the luck that got you here in the first place.

Most guys went through stages like that but Sprinkles didn't. Sprinkles went from innocence, awkwardness, and fear to utter calm under fire and utter competence without somehow ever bothering to leave the innocence behind. Outside the sweeps you could count on him to do the crazy thing, the thing nobody else would do anymore. He was the one to pet the dog, to feed the kid, to learn the language so he could talk to papa-san and mama-san. A perennial newboots, just jumped out of the chopper.

He always had to get in close, he thought. I always had to watch him.

And now he thought about him a lot these days. Maybe it was just that the last of his own innocence was gone, with Alma and the boy gone now, and thinking of Sprinkles was mourning it somehow. He didn't know.

He turned the rabbit again. It was almost done.

He drank the whiskey. It was getting dark but the ground was warm from the sun. On a day like this in Nam—a day you had sun—the night would come in so cold and fast you lay down if you could to suck the heat from the earth like a sponge.

He'd have dinner, he thought, he'd eat, then maybe put some music on and kill the bottle. Why not. There was no one around to worry about anymore.

Chapter Eight

"Good god," she said aloud, "the woods!"

Caroline turned off the shower and reached for the body oil, poured some into the palm of her hand and began smoothing it over her skin. The light, sweet, nutty scent of sesame seed pleased her. I must be diseased, she thought. I *like* a shower. I like to be soft and warm and clean. For three whole days she was going to be none of these. She was going to be dirty and there would be bugs and god knows what crawling, buzzing things and a foam mattress on the hard cold ground. I have a mental disease, she thought. I am nuts and this week we have nature asylum. *Per aspera ad astra* and the boogie-woogie flu.

Of course it was Kelsey's fault. Kelsey was a lovable, tender, brilliant bastard but a bastard nonetheless—sired, if she had to make a guess, by Catastrophe. On Prestidigitation. She swore that the man could find and inhabit an Extreme Position faster than any man alive, could get you in over your public or private head in seconds. Bring Kelsey to a party and he was sure to tweak a client or two, a host or hostess, or hell, a whole roomful of clients, within the first twenty minutes—talk Nazis to a Jew or Freud to a WASP or the perversions of Christ to either of them. Take him to an airport and half an hour later he'd have you skydiving.

It was just that kind of life. In 1969 he'd arranged to cover the war in Vietnam for the Boston *Herald,* and forget that it had been dangerous, forget that he'd been shot at a number of times, forget that he'd flown to Saigon just one week after his arrest at a Cambridge peace demonstration. It had also been smart. Because his resulting first novel about the Saigon journalists' corps, *Response to Impact,* had won him the Pulitzer Prize. That was smart.

But he'd also hunted rattlesnakes in Texas and alligators in Louisiana swamps and damn near gotten bit by both of them, he'd trekked the Mojave Desert and white water rafted the Colorado, climbed three or four mountains, jumped off cliffs with aluminum gliders and yes, parachuted out of actual moving airplanes (and *paid* to do these things)! He'd cried all night at Esalen back in '70 and sat in Brazilian coke-bars and Haitian bordellos and had probably tried every drug and alcoholic beverage known to man. Worse, he'd attacked senators, congressmen, an ex-president, a TV glamour queen and half the writers and critics in New York City in cold print—and all this had won him nothing as far as she could see except a reputation for biohazard.

Then, of course, there were the affairs.

Her husband had no death wish that she was aware of, but he was definitely attracted to things that were uncomfortable and hopelessly male and dangerous at times, so that camping in the woods—even with his mistress along—was at least working toward the uncomfortable side of his predispositions rather than the outright lethal. So she supposed she could deal with the gnats and spiders.

And what could you do? If you loved him, what could you do?

She thought about Michelle.

What indeed.

She took a towel off the rack and patted dry so as not to smear away the sesame oil. I smell like a plate of Szechuan peanut noodles, she thought. She stepped from the tub into the warm directional lighting and had a look at herself in the mirror.

I was never a beautiful woman, she thought. But at age forty-five there is class to this package. Droop, but also class. Even stark naked it's there. Just let me loose on Rodeo Drive with a charge card or two and I'll show you what taste can do for class, and conversely.

She took another towel off the rack and bent to towel-dry her hair. She was letting it grow in longer these days, longer than it had been since she was a girl, so she wrapped it when she was through and walked barefoot to the bedroom. Downstairs she could hear Kelsey at the IBM Selectric in the study. She supposed it was the novel. You had to give it to him, the man worked very hard. She wondered if it was going well. She frowned. She suspected it still wasn't.

She went to the closet and exchanged the towel for a plain terry cloth robe and dropped the towel on the big four-poster bed. At the mirror she plugged in the dryer and began to blow-dry her hair. The sound of it buried the typing downstairs and that was good. Kelsey was obliterated for a moment. She stared into the mirror.

I've got myself a problem, she thought.

Face it. You may be fighting for your life here.

It had been Monday afternoon that Michelle said she was pregnant, and she was amazed at her reaction, amazed that she felt no anger, no betrayal, not even jealousy over the fact that Michelle *was* pregnant while Caroline could not be, not ever—no, she was only surprised that the girl had chosen her to talk to about it, though she supposed, later, that it made good sense in a way, surprised and then aware of a slowly rising sense of panic, of dread, as it dawned on her once and for all that of all the women Kelsey had been involved with over the years *this* was the one to be afraid of.

It was not just the pregnancy. That was only the final piece to the picture of Michelle and Kelsey that had been forming in her mind for months. It was a picture she'd built growing friendly with Michelle, doing her usual (natural for her, if otherwise admittedly eccentric) thing of keeping an eye on the relationship from the inside—secure in the knowledge that it would take one hell of an extraordinary person to pry Kelsey away from her—reassuring Michelle that she was welcome in their lives because Kelsey seemed to need and want her there and that she was not one to suffer jealousy, that in fact Caroline liked her too. Then soon it was a picture of Michelle as a woman, gradually revealed to her—smart, sexy, funny, considerate, loving, loyal, tough, successful as hell, and undeniably decent. Also twenty years her junior and light-years more beautiful. Extraordinary? What else did you need to qualify?

There had always been the urge to protect the others somehow. No matter how good Kelsey's taste had been—and it was good—or how strong the women, she had known that unless it was strictly fun and games for them they would always get the bad end sooner or later. On occasions she'd even helped him work it out so as to leave them, when he had to, with their dignity intact. Knowing her husband was making love to other women was one thing; thinking that he might be screwing them was another. Kelsey was as good as men come, she supposed, but that was still a very long way from perfect. It wasn't always easy to do. The women were vulnerable almost by definition. Because the end had always been a foregone conclusion. Kelsey came home.

Michelle was different. Michelle *was* a kind of home for Kelsey. She knew it. She could see it in the ease and intimacy between them. In some ways it reminded her of hers with Kelsey. In other respects it was distinctively their own. And more and more often lately Caroline found reason to suspect that Michelle in her way was every bit as good for him as she herself was. Apart from his professional worries—and they were impressive worries—Kelsey was clearly happy. Together they looked and felt committed, like this was definitely going to be around awhile. So finally the picture of Kelsey and Michelle together that emerged for her was a picture of success. Emotional, physical (and hell, why not say it), even spiritual success. And Caroline was not part of it. Not necessarily.

So she'd almost spilled her coffee when Michelle had leaned across the table at Ma Maison and said she was pregnant, and that final piece went *click!* into place. She can have babies, she thought. Kelsey doesn't know it yet but he will want them and she can have them.

She felt a sudden roll of nausea and it was definitely not in sympathy with anybody's goddamn morning sickness.

She rallied quickly. But all the rest of the day she couldn't get her hands warm for constantly wanting to wring them. Or wring their necks.

Her response, though, was open and instinctive.

I know a doctor, she said. He's an old, old friend and he'll be very careful to be discreet. We'll handle it between us. You'll tell Kelsey when it's over and no-body need ever know.

She'd ridden to the rescue. Wonderful.

She'd called that evening and made an appointment with the doctor. Still in utter empathy with the woman even though the fear had never left her. And it was only then that she realized completely the craziness of what she'd done, that she'd just arranged an abortion for her husband's lover. His extraordinary, dangerous lover. A short while later she realized that it was possible to hate a woman you thoroughly respected and liked. And finally she realized what she had here—that she was easily able to destroy this woman with a simple phone call to the L.A. *Herald Examiner.*

Just check the doctor's clinic schedule for Friday the 26th, please. That's right, Dr. Phillip Geis. G-E-I-S. He's in the book. Two thirty P.M. Thank you. Bye.

It could be done.

It would be strictly evil. There was no getting around it.

But you had to see it this way too: there were two ideas in life that she'd simply gotten used to. One was enjoying her profession. The other was living with Bernard J. Kelsey, hopefully to a ripe old rocking-chair age and enjoying that too. They were just about all that mattered to her.

Mess with either one and nothing was exactly out of the question.

She tossed her hair. She supposed it was dry enough. I used to be a completely decent person, she thought. She unplugged the drier, turned down the bed, took off the robe, and slipped naked between the fresh linen sheets. They smelled clean and she thought that maybe, just maybe she might want Kelsey inside her tonight, the sheets felt good—and maybe he'd want her as well. I am in need of reassurance, she told herself, and that would be nice for a change.

Then she wasn't sure again. Sex. My one huge flaw, she thought. It was nobody's fault except maybe her father's, but what could you do, the man was Law and nothing but Law all the way to his coronary and he left me lots of money, at least, but I do wish he'd not felt all that stiff repugnance about touching, I do wish he hadn't left me the other as well. Half the time, sexually, I'd rather be in Cleveland.

She turned her face toward the pillow.

And now maybe I have another flaw. Also huge.

Damn it. This was Kelsey's fault too. Why couldn't the man want beach bunnies and bimbos like half the other writers she knew? Why'd he want to bother with a woman?

I really hope I don't do this to you, Mich, she thought. Honestly. I really hope I don't. But I don't know. I truly wish somebody would tell me not to.

Downstairs the Selectric stopped and fitfully started again, ran hard and fast for a line or two, then paused, a long pause—and the house seemed empty, silent.

CHAPTER NINE

In the dream it was morning and they were coming into the ville where Ragweed had disappeared the night before and it was quiet now, it looked empty but for the smoke from cooking fires, and they were moving toward the hooch where they'd met the little Vietnamese whore.

He was walking point as usual and Sprinkles was walking slack though that was not the way it really was, somewhere inside the dream he was aware of the dislocation, because Scag walked his slack nearly always and Sprinkles was usually at the rear of the column, at drag. But in the dream that was how it was so that when they opened up the hooch it was he and Sprinkles together pointing their rifles at the girl crouched alone inside, impossible to say how old she was except maybe fifteen and maybe twenty, dirty and scared, rightly scared now because Ragweed had gone off alone to her and he had not come back, and all of them knew it.

They walked her out of the hooch and stood her in the dusty flat center of the ville and asked, where's GI? where's GI? and she kept shaking her head, she didn't know, gone sullen ignorant and angry on them, the silly bitch, because they'd been mad enough to kill her on sight just walking into the place, never mind now, but she just kept shaking her head, don't know. And people were coming out of the other hooches, mostly women and kids and a couple old papa-sans, watching them timidly, a pretty good number of people in that ville, and Henderson said, fuck this, let's look around. If it moves, shoot it.

So that then (and this was not the way it happened either, because it was Doc who found him) they walked behind the hooches and there was what was left of Ragweed propped up in the grass, sitting on top of a stone like some kind of sick roadside shrine, a black man's head with black-red sockets where the eyes had been and his dick shoved into his open mouth.

Sprinkles turned and puked, a long red arc into the grass—and then suddenly they were back inside the girl's hooch, trashing it, looking for VC papers because they knew she was Cong by then, she had to be, trashing the hooch while Henderson and Clemons beat the hell out of the naked whore, screaming at her, furious, all the months of the fear and tension of the sweeps exploding in them, wanting to know where her buddies were—a VC finally, *finally* in hand and not sniping out of spider holes or mining trails or sliding into camp at night to slit their throats—Henderson and Clemons holding her down while Semple used his boot knife on her face and breasts and kicked her and finally edged the muzzle of his M16 up into her snatch all this happening fast, fast in the dream—screaming at her, the girl screaming back, the whole hooch dripping with rage and agony.

Then the blurt of Semple's rifle and the splash of bright blood, her body trembling, jerking, and Doc yelling, hey, look at this! look at this! over here! so they do look, and he's over in the far corner of the hooch, the hooch in the dream taking on ten more yards of depth suddenly, but they go to him, they leave the dead whore's body and they see that Doc has pulled back the grass on the floor in front of him and uncovered a square trapdoor made of old weathered wood.

Silently they group together and stare down at the trap. They look at one another. Sprinkles's face has turned a sickly white. Semple is grinning strangely. Lee bends down to take hold of the door. His fingers close hard on the wood. He takes a deep breath and holds it. The other men step back, all but Sprinkles. Lee is scared as hell. He wrenches the door away . . .

The AK-47 fire tears suddenly through the thatched roof, whines past his ear, into the night and out of the dream as Lee falls away. He rolls for his M16 but it's not there, rolls into cups and stacks of books, comes up against an empty bottle. He reaches into his boot for the five-inch knife, pulls it free of its sheath, comes up into a crouch. He stares wide-eyed some fifteen degrees to the left of the opening of his tent so its image hits the side of his retina where the black-and-white receptor rods are located. He can smell his own sweat.

He listens, frozen, ready to leap sideways or on through the tent opening as the case may be. Something moves outside and he tenses. Where are the others? he wonders. They've got to hear it too. It's big. Man-sized. He can hear it moving.

The sweat slides down across his naked chest, turns his genitals clammy, runs down into his eyes. He blinks it away.

The sound banks off to the left. Farther. Farther. Still farther. Okay, fine, it's far enough now. Slowly, soundlessly he edges toward the opening. He peers around the flap, to the left, to the right. The movement is toward the right. It stops and starts, stops and starts. He can't hear it now. He crawls from the tent like a spider to the ashes of his campfire, past it, into the brush. He settles in beyond the perimeter and waits.

The movements seem to reverse themselves. They're coming toward him, working around the brush at the edges of the clearing. He presses flat to the ground, fucks the dirt. The movements are just to his left now, almost close enough for him to use the knife but not yet, not yet, hold on just a moment—and then they're practically right on top of him, he can come up out of the brush and slit the bastard's throat right now, right now, it's perfect, the knife is up and ready and he is ready too.

And then he stops. Realizes what he's listening to.

He wonders, where's the dog?

Not a twig cracks or a leaf rustles as he rises up into a crouch again and peers beyond the brush.

A pair of eyes pool starlight toward him. Not three feet away. It isn't the dog. The dog has been ranging far afield again.

While the doe has been feeding. Now she stares at Lee in amazement, a look of wild, intense curiosity, a kind of wonder at finding him there. Lee stares back, relief spilling through him like a drug. She is four feet tall and near enough to touch. Her coat is a rich textured brown, spotted white. Her eyes hold him hypnotized. Beautiful eyes. The most beautiful eyes he's ever seen. He wants to touch her.

He tries to hold her with his eyes. Slowly he raises his hand. She doesn't seem to notice. She's focused on his eyes even as the hand reaches out to her, moving steadily, evenly, a slow, controlled, open-handed glide until he's merely inches from her neck and still she stares—and he can hardly help it, he starts to smile as the fingertips taste the thick smooth fur, even the warmth of her for a moment before he thinks, the eyes, my god, the eyes, they remind me of the eyes of children.

It brings back the dream.

The children. He sees them. Their eyes now in hers. And he thinks, poor Sprinkles.

The doe can feel the change, she can see this memory in him like a fire in the brush and as his fingers reach out to touch her, press gently toward the living warmth of her, she suddenly senses death in him. Her eyes blink once, astounded.

She runs. Across the brook. Deep into the forest and hard into the night.

"Alma," he says.

91

—Part Two—

Chapter Ten

The black stretch limo pulled into the driveway as tentatively as a drunk the morning after a bender. "Would you look at that," Kelsey said to Caroline. "Walker made it."

It was just over an hour past dawn and they were packing the Jeep. The tents were already inside, as were the packs and sleeping bags, the hiking boots, and lantern. The Jeep was looking serious now. Kelsey hauled up a box of supplies.

"Alan!"

Kelsey wiped his hands on his jeans and walked to the limousine. The driver already had the door open. Alan Walker swung out, smiling, looking better in denim jeans and a work shirt than a man of fifty had any right to expect. They shook hands. The driver handed Walker a dark leather clothes-bag.

"Alan, you made it."

"Of course I made it. You invited me, didn't you?"

He indicated the bag. "I hope this isn't going to be a problem."

"Not so long as you don't mind a scratch or two."

"That's all right."

He waved to Caroline and dismissed the driver. The limousine pulled carefully back out of the driveway. For a moment he seemed to study Kelsey, then put a hand on his shoulder. They walked to the Jeep.

Caroline smiled and gave Alan a hug. "Hello, beautiful," she said.

He laughed. "Caroline, the ego just soars."

"Can I get you some coffee?"

"You certainly can."

"Bernie?"

"I'll finish here. You two go ahead."

Caroline took Alan's arm and they walked toward the house, already talking business.

Kelsey threw another box into the Jeep. He saw that Caroline had straightened up a bit. She and Walker, he thought, they're a lot alike. Organized and appropriate in a way I'll never be. In effect they were competitors yet he'd never once seen competition between them. Not even when some client bounced from one agency to the other, as now and then happened. They seemed to understand one another too well for that. Walker had been his agent for ten years now. His agent and his friend—and his wife's friend too. It was something rare in the publishing world, their friendship. Though Caroline's expertise was largely in movies while Alan's was books, that should not have stopped them from casually disliking each other the way everyone else in the business seemed to do.

That had never been the case, though. Especially after Alan's wife had died of cancer three years ago, after a long hard bout with it, so hard it had turned his hair white in a single year, he and Caroline had gotten closer and closer until Kelsey wondered, sometimes, what would happen between them if he himself were to die. And it was comforting, actually, to think about that.

He broke open the shotguns and checked them, then set them into the wall rack. There was one for him and an extra for Walker. Two Browning Citori 20-gauge over-and-under firearms, first barrel modified for scatter-shot and the second full-choke for long-range shooting. Ross would bring his own weapon and neither Caroline nor Michelle did any shooting. That would leave the kid from *Rolling Stone*—what was his name, Graham? He supposed Graham would be content just to use his camera. There were quail and pheasant in the scrub and he'd even heard of people bagging wild turkey now and then.

The bathroom window was open and he heard the shower go off inside, which meant that Michelle would be nearly ready. That was good. Assuming Ross and Graham arrived on time they could leave within the hour. Michelle had been up well before dawn in order to get in her morning workout, Walker was here, and they were packed and ready.

A weekend in the woods, he thought. Three days off from that damned, damned book. He closed the Jeep doors and went inside for coffee.

Walter Graham's Rent-a-Wreck Dodge Aspen whined along at sixty miles per hour behind Kelsey's Jeep and the sporty red Mercedes. He was not entirely sure his car had ever bothered to pick up third gear. Or maybe it had just skipped second. He didn't know. He wasn't too much of a driver. Kelsey, it appeared, could really handle the Jeep on the throughways, even loaded and unwieldy as it was, and sometimes it was hard keeping up with them.

No problem, he thought. I'm a fucking bloodhound here.

I smell gorgeous pictures.

Back home in Seattle he'd jumped at this assignment—hell, he had to, it was a stringer's dream. They'd wanted a guy who'd shot both news and per-sonality as well as plenty of nature stuff, and he was the guy. Oh yes he was. Never mind that the pay was only fair to middling—they were willing to import him. Never mind that he hadn't even read the Nick Tosches interview by then, though he'd done so later on the plane, and thought it was pretty good, actually, pretty provocative. It was Kelsey. It was Kelsey that excited him. Kelsey whom he'd read for ten years now, from *Response to Impact* back in high school and the Hollywood novel *Simple Gifts* in college to *Out of Our Hands,* which he was sure was the god-damnedest greatest piece of nonfiction writing he'd ever read or ever fucking *would* read, and finally *Dou-ble Veteran* and if the critics and half the women in the country had trounced on that one, well, Graham himself had wanted to stand up and cheer. The point was that Graham knew his subject. He knew his point of view. And he knew exactly how he wanted to photograph him.

And then to arrive at the Bel Air house and meet

him, see the ease of the guy, the grace of the guy, the charm of the guy, plus the sheer photogenic *quality* of each and every one of them, then to realize immediately that he was in the middle of an intrigue here too and maybe even a couple of them, because it was not just the Kelsey-Caroline-Michelle Ryan triangle that was going down here, he knew a little about that from the Tosches interview, no; the agent Alan Walker was looking pretty strained if you had the eyes to pick up on it, troubled somehow, there was something going on between him and Kelsey though god knew what but dammit, he was taking bets he'd find out, and finally there was Ross, the playwright, also good for the shoot, handsome in his way, a good weak empty face to contrast with the rest of them, clearly nobody's buddy but Kelsey's and even that maybe open to question—to arrive in the midst of all this was to know you had *story* as well as subject, and you had to be open to anything.

Ahead of him Kelsey turned off the throughway into the hills. Ross's red Mercedes followed him closely and farther back, so did Graham, who smiled, slapped the heel of his hand against the steering wheel in time to the Thompson Twins' tune on the radio.

Kelsey A goddamn genius in turmoil in a pastoral setting.

He'd get work out of this, lots of work. He knew it. He couldn't believe his luck.

The elements were all there. The cameras, the perfect photographer, the subject, the place, story, props, and the supporting cast of characters. Even the day was coming up big and clear.

The moments, the pictures would be there too.
It was just a feeling but dammit, he trusted it.
It was going to be a hell of a shoot.

The campsite was a clearing on a hill surrounded by
tall stands of pine.

It was Kelsey who knew the place, he'd been here
three years ago with Mailer and some other hotshot
novelist, and Ross had not been invited that time because Mailer, the asshole, didn't like him. Kelsey had
not told him but it was nothing new to Ross, not being liked, and he knew the signs. For one thing the
day they met at Scribner's in New York and then
went out to lunch the Great Man's handshake was
limp. Here's Mailer, this macho tough guy who wrote
The Naked and the Dead for chrissake greeting him
with a limp fist. Ross hadn't a chance. Not a single
goddamn chance. One good look and it's like old Ross
is just dead meat. And the rest of the afternoon he's
joking around with Kelsey and having a merry time
and what does Ross get? Mailer's *nice* to him. The
condescending prick. He'd read the stage version of
The Deer Park and Mailer couldn't write a play to save
his nuts from the meatman. The asshole.

Ross was a poet. Mailer just wrote stories.

The thought of the three-year-old insult had his
face flushing. So cool it, he thought. Cool it now. All
that's past. All gone now.

Because here he was with the rest of them standing
at the top of the hill looking down over a wide pond
of clear still water, birds swooping down across it to

the surrounding trees. And Mailer, the rat-sucking reamed-out bastard, was not present.

". . . there's nothing very much in there, though," Kelsey was saying. "At least there wasn't last time. Somebody got the bright idea that it'd make for better fishing to stock it up with trout, when there were plenty of bass already. So the trout killed off the bass population just like they were supposed to do. But they hadn't taken the water temperature into account. Nobody thought of that. A trout's a cold-water fish. The water was much too warm for the trout so they died too. What you've got down there now is the memory of a pretty healthy fishing hole."

"Looks fine for swimming, though," said Michelle.

"Should be."

"I can get in my laps. Good."

"That you can."

It looked okay to Ross as well. All told, a pretty decent campsite—if you liked camping. Good level ground carpeted with pine needles, so sleep shouldn't be too hard, especially with the foam floormats. There would be cool fresh water from the feeder streams, according to Kelsey, and the hilltop sat high enough to be away from some of the insects. Plenty of shade from the pine trees when you wanted it and plenty of sun on the site itself. He could firm up the tan, maybe. Hell, they were all alone up here. There wasn't another camper in sight. He could do a little skinny-dipping down at the pond at night. Maybe convince Caroline or Michelle to join him.

Oh yeah. Lots of luck there, he thought.

There was a whole cardboard box filled with vodka, scotch, wines and mixers in the Jeep though. So that maybe if you lubricated things a little. You never knew. People did all kinds of weird things in fresh air.

"I guess we should start unpacking," said Caroline.

"We should," said Kelsey. "We should get the tents up, anyway."

Kelsey'd told him pretty much what to buy, and he'd stowed most of it in the Jeep—though the side-by-side 20-bore shotgun he'd left on the floor of the Mercedes, it just felt good there so that now, since he was last to arrive at the house in Bel Air, his own stuff came out first. The goose-down sleeping bag with the water-repellent shell, the big external-frame pack, the lightweight hiking boots. He chose a spot close to the trail leading down to the water. They hauled out the boxes of supplies, the axe, and the lantern, and piled them where the fire would be. Then they pulled out the tents, three of them—one for Michelle and Caroline, one for Kelsey and Alan Walker, and a third for him and Graham. Figures, he thought, that he'd get the kid photographer. He guessed somebody had to. The tents were all heat-resistant nylon, double-walled, with taped-seam bathtub floors, shock-corded aluminum poles and no-see-um netted doors and windows. State of the art and a lot more expensive than Ross would have wished, though he'd never have said that to Kelsey.

Still, they'd be comfortable.

He checked his watch. Close to eleven.

It was a bright, warm day.

Okay, he thought, let's get this damn thing up.

"Hey Graham." The kid was unloading his cameras. "How about a little help here."

He peeled off his shirt and set it on top of his pack.

He walked to the tent. He could see his reflection in the new aluminum tubing. It was a damn good body.

And Norman bloody Mailer didn't have that, either.

CHAPTER ELEVEN

When finally he DEROSed to Fort Lewis, Washington, they flew him home on a C-141 transport stacked with GI coffins—the KIA Travel Bureau they called it, flights daily out of Graves Registration. It was so damn cold up there you couldn't smell the stink. One day he's in Nam, coming out of a hot LZ in a light chopper, antiaircraft fire all around, and the next night he's standing in a Seattle bar. Just like that. It's winter and he's the only one in the place with a tan. He's short-haired and conspicuous. Women are looking at him. Men with beards and jesus-cuts are looking at him. Nobody's friendly. He orders a beer and a shot of whiskey and listens to the music. He drinks the beer and the whiskey but it doesn't help, he doesn't feel right in there, he looks down and his hands are trembling. He goes outside for a cigarette. On the stoop he lights the cigarette and tosses away the match and suddenly he feels a hand grip his shoulder. In the dark he re-acts instinctively.

He whirls and swings. Both hands, cupped, slapping the ears, an open palm breaking the nose, a forearm to the trachea, a quick half turn and an elbow into the sternum.

He looks at the guy. The guy is bleeding and can hardly breathe.

Seconds tick by and Lee is in trouble and all he can do is look.

He probably needed a match, he thinks.

It's like that now.

The dog's wet nose at his neck propels him out of bed and that's twice, goddammit, in just twelve hours.

Jesus!

The dog is looking up at him, used to him by now and not at all perplexed by his behavior. Smiling in fact, the pink tongue amiably lolling.

"For chrissakes, dog!"

The dog backs up and waits for him outside the tent. He squints through the opening. It's bright out there. Real bright. He walks outside, looks at the sky.

Noon.

How the hell he's slept till noon he doesn't know. As far as he can remember it's the first time he's done it in years. Never before in the jungle—in the woods. Not since the day I walked, he thought.

It feeds off the earlier memory. Because after the business at the bar he'd run away, caught a bus back to camp, and nobody ever did find out that it was Lee who'd put the man in the hospital, so they shipped him to California for his tail-of-the-dog tour, all mickey mouse horseshit like you wouldn't believe, as though he'd never been to Nam and killed and damn near died and was still about to care when they pulled their Rear Echelon Mother Fucker nonsense on him, as though he was supposed to put up with all their drill and shoe polish like a lifer. He'd taken it for one month exactly until he was able to manage a two-day leave and then packed a bag and walked out of there forever, AWOL, an outlaw, a wanted man—and the following afternoon he'd awakened in a cheap hotel in San Francisco. It was noon by the hotel clock and he'd never slept so well in his life nor wakened so scared and angry.

And now he was angry too, though it was nothing to the other, nothing so basic as feeling pissed at ninety-nine percent of the population of North America. Who were they to drill him? Who were they, at the bar, to gawk at him like somebody's latest mouth disease? No, this was anger at himself. He'd slept through half the day and he wanted a deer today, a big six-point buck that would feed them for a while. It was illegal but so was everything else he was doing here.

He thought about the doe.

"Where the fuck were you last night?" he said to the dog. For that matter, he thought, where you been this morning?

"Worthless shit."

The dog, watching him, happy to be spoken to, pranced once around the long-dead coals of the camp-fire. Lee watched him. He felt the anger dissipate. Probably fed himself, he thought. He's a good dog.

"Want to hunt?" he said.

It was a phrase the dog knew. His eyes brightened. He looked at Lee and barked, looked and barked again.

"Okay," he said, "Coffee first. Shave maybe." He felt his beard, thought of the water in the stream. It would be cold.

"Nah. Skip the shave."

The dog barked a third time.

"Enough now."

The dog settled back onto his haunches. A garter snake moved in the scrub nearby. The dog took note of it.

Lee kicked down the ashes of yesterday's campfire, spread them flat, walked to the pile of kindling and began carrying it over—and that was when they heard the shot. A single loud report, a shotgun.

The dog stood up and cocked his head, excited.

A mile away, Lee guessed it was, in the direction of Basker's Pond. He stood motionless. He listened for anything else. M60s, Ml6s. Carbines.

A second report sounded—a shotgun again.

The day was still and clear.

He began to sweat.

You fuckers, he thought, leave me alone.

The dog looked at him, questioning.

He put down the kindling and crouched beside it, listening.

CHAPTER TWELVE

"That's good," said Kelsey, putting down the axe. Ross stood grinning at him, the shotgun smoking a little. "You blasted the side of a tree. Also you just scared away every living thing for miles. Very good."

"Just wanted to get the feel of the thing. I haven't shot for years."

He glanced at Michelle by the tent, holding her ears.

"You have the feel of it now?"

"She kicks."

"Eh?"

"The gun. She kicks."

"Shotguns do. How about a hand here."

"Sure."

"Hatchet's over there. If you quarter some of the smaller ones it'd be helpful. You hurt that tree, you know."

"Nah."

"Yeah. You did."

Why was it, Kelsey wondered, that if there was something someone could do in any given situation that was one-hundred percent sure to irritate the majority of those present, Ross always found it. He could be counted upon to be inappropriate—to say the wrong thing, do the wrong thing, spill the red drink on the white rug or sneeze into the cocaine. The man had the social skills of a hornet. Oh, Kelsey himself had been known to prick the odd bourgeois now and then—it kept you mentally fit if your antagonist was worth a damn and it was always done with calculation. But he really didn't think Ross was aware of what he was doing half the time—most of the time.

He'd always felt there were two basic types of self-consciousness. One—the more familiar—kept you shy, sent you so deeply into yourself that it was impossible to believe that everyone, everywhere was not watching you constantly, judging you, and of course, finding you wanting. The other type sent you just as deeply inward, made you just as thin-skinned to slight or insult, but here you did the judging, and it was impossible to believe that everyone everywhere was not blind as a mole, probably irrelevant to you at best and at worst utterly rotten. Both imposed a kind of tyranny on anyone who wasn't afflicted with that kind of total self-absorption—the first passive, obliging the world to defend itself continually against charges of cruelty to so sensitive a creature as you and the second aggressive, a grand inflated bull in the china shop of human consciousness and human life. Neither type could see to the depth of a pinprick into anyone but themselves, but in themselves saw worlds of pain and potential glory.

Ross was the latter type, the bull—and for years, despite himself, Kelsey had been chief picador. He knew that, and he also knew there wasn't much to be done about it. Except, as Caroline kept urging him to do, to drop the man completely.

The problem was he owed Ross.

It wasn't something Caroline would understand readily. Her decisions about people were as practical and unsentimental as her business decisions. Where she saw worth or merit, she valued. Where she saw little, she cast aside. Life, she said, was busy enough already.

That was true but it was also true that he owed the man.

"Shit!" said Ross. "Ugh!" He was quartering a length of pine and he'd peeled the bark away, and there were termites there.

"Throw it away."

Ross smiled. "What the hell. Burn the little bastards."

"The wood's old. All you'll get is smoke. You don't want it, believe me."

He shrugged. "Right."

To Kelsey's other side Alan Walker glanced at him and smiled, working up a sweat with his axe on a stack of white pine. Kelsey had most of the hardwoods they'd found and there weren't many of them. A few oak logs to burn slowly overnight. But it was mostly fir, pine, and scrub out here. They'd have to gather more again tomorrow. He smelled his hands. Pine sap. Tart and sweet. A long time since he'd smelled that.

"I'm just wondering," said Ross. "Is there some sort of plan?"

"Plan?"

"Order of business. Stuff we have to do yet."

"No. Not once this is finished. Tents are all up,

food's unpacked. Caroline and Michelle were pretty quick about getting the beer into the water. As soon as we've got the wood, we're done. I know Graham wants some pictures but he can do that no matter what we're into, so it's up to you."

"I thought I'd take a swim, maybe."

"Sure, why not."

"Where'd he go, anyway?"

"Graham? Back over the hill into the woods there. Scouting locations I guess. Something."

"You see the interview yet?"

"No."

"You ask to?"

"No."

"Why not?"

"I was there. I said it. I don't need to read it."

"You trust them?"

"I didn't say that. What's to trust? Either they get it right or they don't. If they don't, I sue them."

Ross shook his head. "Jesus, Bernie. I don't get you, I really don't. By then the damage is done. Damned if I'd let them print an interview with me without a preview copy."

They didn't ask you for one, thought Kelsey.

And then he thought, I'm being pretty unkind.

But the fact was that they never would. Ross wasn't news anymore, and only briefly had he ever been. One big play that Papp had taken from the Public to Broadway six years ago, and then another one two years later that had folded and died in a single week, both of them sharply clever and abstract and both of them, in Kelsey's opinion, all talk and no soul, the difference between them being that whereas the first had featured a particularly brutal onstage rape the second had not and thus died in search of a sensation.

Ross was talented, there was no denying that, with a fine ear for syntax and a better sense than his own for formal structure. But he had no grasp of the reasons people did things—even simple motives were a mystery to him as were the interactions, the loves and hates which over the years tended to form them. The conflicts in his plays were always arbitrary, counterfeit, inhuman somehow—even his rapist raped not out of lust or rage but out of some abstract principle of will or alienation or relativity, Kelsey forgot which—they were conflicts no more substantial than two shadows crossing on a city street.

He respected the plays formally and cared for them not at all.

And he knew his own success grated at Ross, absolutely galled him.

He had come to success, in Ross's opinion, the easy way. And in a way it was true. The jobs had always been there, the doors opened at every turn—he was writing for *Boston After Dark* before he finished college and the first job he applied for after that, with the Boston *Herald,* was given to him on the spot. While Ross struggled through a succession of odd jobs to support his playwriting Kelsey went to war and then wrote about it and fashioned a career practically overnight. That it had taken a reasonable skill and plenty of hard work, that it had destroyed more than one important relationship entirely and shortened a slew of others both before and after Caroline meant nothing whatsoever to

Ross, because the success was undeniably there. Measured against Ross's own, Kelsey had paid insufficient dues and that was that.

Divorced, childless, Ross clearly envied Kelsey his relationship with Caroline, too, and did little to disguise the fact. Now there was Michelle. Kelsey wondered how he was dealing with that.

Still he owed the man.

They fell silent for a while and he thought about that.

"Finished."

Ross tossed down the hatchet and lifted a load of split wood, carried it to where they were stacking it just beyond the tents. Then he came back for a second load.

"You think your friend would go if I asked her?" he said.

"You mean Mich? Where, swimming?"

"Yeah."

"Might. She likes to swim."

"Okay, I'll ask her. You mind?"

"Mind? God no."

"Okay, I'll ask her."

He walked to the tents. Across from Kelsey Alan Walker was grinning again. Now Kelsey smiled too.

"Alan, do me a favor and stuff it, will you?"

He laughed. "I just hope she doesn't drown him."

Kelsey brought down the axe, a good clean split. The wood fell away.

That, he guessed, was how Ross was dealing with Michelle. What else had he expected?

His debt to Ross went all the way back to college,

to his sophomore year, when first his father and then, four months later, his mother had died of heart attacks, the busy Long Island soda shop and luncheonette they'd owned all his life having finally taken theirs. Ross had been his roommate then, had loaned him money and listened through those long Back Bay winter nights while he talked about his parents, the constant bickering that drove him off to college in the first place, their thwarted attempts at reconciliation, and all that remained unsaid between them and now would forever remain unsaid.

Proximity, youth, books made up their bond, and the fact that, insofar as an early harvest of suffering went, with a drunken mother and an abusive father back home, Ross's family life was more than a match for his own. And it lasted. Ross was younger then, less bitter than sardonic and far more optimistic. Of the two of them it was he and not Kelsey who could be relied upon to pull them out of their black moods to a dance or a bar or a movie. As a writer he had always been a prodigy. By graduation he was ready to conquer the world—or at least the American theater. And he supported Kelsey's own writing like a teacher with a promising student. It was condescending. He knew that now. But more than anything or anybody else, it got him started.

He had long since paid back the money, but he could never pay off those long nights talking or that early support at a time when he was drifting and support was so lacking. He knew that Ross today was not a likable man. His years of struggle, his moderate success and then, more recently, his total lack of it were driving him steadily crazy, in Kelsey's opinion. The prognosis was not good. Youth and optimism were no longer there to head off the anger or the self-destructiveness. The snake was eating its tail, producing nothing. He doubted that Ross had finished even a one-act play in three years. He doubted he'd been in love for a great deal longer than that.

And where could you get without love?

"What do you think, Alan," he said. "Have we got enough here?"

The shade had shifted. They were standing in bright sunlight now and both men were sweating.

"Plenty, it seems to me."

"Me too," he said.

They gathered up the firewood and walked back into camp. The women were sitting on a pair of stumps, talking and drinking Pepsi. Ross, he guessed, had had to swim alone.

CHAPTER THIRTEEN

Graham heard the first shot and turned in the direction of the camp, wondering if it was intended as some sort of signal to him. He'd come a ways farther than he meant to but a forest would do that to him, like some overland case of oxygen narcosis—he kept wanting to go deeper.

You can take the kid out of the woods, he thought, but you can't kid the woods out of the . . . something.

The second shot sounded. He listened. SOS was three. Kelsey would know that.

But the third shot never came.

He kept going.

He was good at this. He was traveling west now down the side of a hill, into thicker scrub than they had up at the campsite, but there were plenty of trees along the way and he kept blazing them with his knife, one cut on each side, with the higher of the two on the side nearer camp just in case he got turned around somehow. In Washington, growing up, he'd had deep woods climbing right up into his backyard. Woods were woods no matter where you were and he still had his skills.

He wasn't sure what he was looking for, exactly—if he was looking for anything at all. The campsite and the pond were both perfectly good locations, as was the big bare granite outcrop just to the north of camp and the clearing he'd just come through a hundred yards back or so. He could get what he needed practically anywhere. So he supposed that what he was doing here was just playing.

And that was fine too.

Why would you want to shoot pictures for a living if you'd given up playing?

He moved down the hill through a stand of low thin oak, then into more scrub. It was steeper here so he walked sideways across the downgrade. The Nikon, suspended from around his neck, thumped against his sternum. The light-weight hiking boots felt comfortable and well seasoned.

The hill dropped off further. He stopped a moment and caught his breath. The air was thicker here, heavy with heat and moisture. He blazed the fir tree beside him and then leaned back against it, peering down into the shallow ravine.

And thought: *What the hell?*

The ravine was choked with vegetation but he had good eyes and a pretty fair notion of what belonged here and what didn't. And this didn't.

Wait a minute. Check this closer, he thought.

He popped the lens cap off the Nikon and brought the camera to his eye, twisted the long 300mm lens and pulled it up into focus. He looked down the hill and a little to the left. The familiar saw-leaf blade bobbed at him, waving in a tiny gust of wind.

I'll be goddamned, he thought. We got us some farmers here.

A vegetable stand.

He wondered if they might not object to sharing a bud or two with the pride of *Rolling Stone,* not to mention *Outdoor Life* (and whoever else his agent could hustle), who also happened to be an aficionado. Of course they wouldn't.

He wouldn't tell them.

He slipped the Nikon under his armpit for safety, sheathed the knife and slid down the hill, and saw where a trail had been worn away leading into the gully, evidence that somebody had been tending their crop pretty regularly. He stopped and listened.

Birds overhead. Insects. That was all.

He stepped out onto the trail.

He could count them now as he approached, fifteen of them, big suckers, taller than the surrounding vegetation by at least a couple of feet or so— fourteen, maybe sixteen feet high. And still growing, he thought. Nobody's going to miss a few buds on these babies.

He bet they were all females. Their color was beautiful. You wouldn't want to risk the quality of a crop as good as this with male plants in there to pollinate them, turning their energy toward nourishing the fertilized seeds, lowering the potency of the leaves. No way. You got them growing this good you knew what you were doing.

You knew all about it.

He was close now.

And yes, they were females all right. He could almost taste them. And he *could* smell them. In the damp heat their familiar spicy tang rode high above the other smells.

He was ten feet away from the first of them.

He walked slowly, steadily. Listening.

Kelsey smoked pot, he remembered. That had come out in the interview. So maybe he'd bring him some.

Sure, he'd bring them a present.

He wondered what Kelsey was like stoned.

His arm swung back against the camera riding near his armpit and he heard the lens cap pop away. At the same time he was aware of something tugging across the front of his left boot, a creeper or something, some hint of resistance there.

"Damn."

He stopped and turned, bending, looked down for the black plastic cap, saw it, then heard something behind him start as a rustle of leaves and change suddenly to something like the sound of a bear bursting toward him through the brush; he felt an electric fear claw across his sweaty back because there *were* bears here, he knew that, felt the blood race suddenly to his head and, as he half turned back toward the sound and the plants something big and hard and hurtful slammed immensely into his shoulder and hurled him back down onto the trail.

Ignoring the pain running all the way down to his wrist he rolled faceup, the naked camera lens digging into the dirt beside him, thinking nothing of that, reaching for the knife, expecting to find himself staring into the eyes of something fanged and huge, red eyed and shaggy coated.

Whereas all he saw, actually, was some well-constructed grill-work.

A flyswatter. Graham the fly.

Son of a bitch.

He picked up the lens cap and hauled himself up to his feet. He scraped the dirt off the camera lens and then had a look at the swatter.

It was very impressive. Had he been facing it directly there was every reason to believe he'd be missing a few teeth and have a broken nose by now.

You got off easy, kid, he thought.

The ache in his arm did nothing to contradict him.

And now it was high time and a good idea to get the hell out of there, before whoever made this ugly little contraption came back for inspection.

But first. *First,* goddammit.

Looking very carefully down at the trail ahead of him he walked to the nearest plant and tore off a handful of buds and leaves. These he stuffed into his pocket.

For Kelsey, he thought.

Kelsey will like this. He'll like the whole damn story, I know he will. Booby traps and farmers—way out here in the middle of nowhere. He'll love it.

And happy now—still scared, shaken, bruised, but really pretty happy—he started back up the hill.

CHAPTER FOURTEEN

"I try to be useful," said Graham.

Kelsey laughed. They were sitting around the campfire, banked with stones. Walker was toasting a hot dog on a stick. Kelsey sniffed the dope again—it smelled good—and passed it over to Ross, who was sitting by Michelle in a pair of wet bikini briefs, a towel draped around his neck. Ross sniffed it too. Michelle peeled an orange. She tossed the peels into the fire.

"And to think," Kelsey said, "that I was wondering about having a photographer along."

"In the woods I'm half bloodhound."

"You could get us back there?"

"Sure I could."

Kelsey thought about it a moment. "I want to see it," he said.

"Thought you might."

"Caroline, pass me one of those dogs and a roll, would you?"

She handed them to him. He threaded the hot dog onto a green peeled branch of wood and held it over the fire.

"Thanks."

"You're welcome. To the hot dog. Not the cannabis." She sat back down again.

Kelsey turned to Graham. "She disapproves."

"Of course I do. I think it's fairly clear that it belongs to somebody who doesn't want visitors."

"I'm not going to steal it, Caroline." He smiled. "Graham's done that already. I just want to see it."

Caroline looked at him. "Bernie, it doesn't *want* to be seen. You know?"

He fixed the smile on her and stared until, in a moment, she smiled too.

"Oh, do what you want," she said. "Personally I wash my hands of you. *Again.*" He laughed.

"That trap," he said to Graham. "It's disarmed now?"

"Uh-huh."

"You sure?"

"I disarmed it the hard way. I'm sure."

"See any others?"

"No."

"And you *would* have seen them, right? Half bloodhound."

Graham nodded. "At least half. Along that approach? Yeah, I think I would have."

"Okay. Let's do it, then. What the hell."

He turned the spitted meat.

"How far?"

"Twenty minutes, roughly."

"I don't suppose you saw any birds along the way."

"Birds?"

"Quail, pheasant. Game birds. You know."

"No."

"Well, we may. Alan? What do you think? Want to take the shotguns?"

Walker shrugged and finished chewing his hot dog. "Can't see why not. There's supposed to be plenty out this way. The only thing is, I wouldn't want to spook anybody."

"You mean whoever owns the plot."

Walker nodded.

"Right," said Kelsey. He thought about it.

"Seems to me," he said, "that if anybody'd been around Graham would have heard about it when he stripped away those leaves. Wouldn't you think? I'd guess it's safe enough. Let's take them. More likely we'd flush a hen than . . . whoever. And then if we *did* run into him and he was really pissed, it might be good to have a little firepower by way of discouragement, right? Make him think about it?"

"Jesus, Kelsey," said Michelle. "What are we doing up here—camping out or playing cowboys and Indians?"

She licked her fingers.

He shrugged. "Little of both," he said. He meant it as a joke but they weren't amused.

"Come on, girls," he said. "Lighten up. I just want to see the damn thing. It'll take us one hour. No more. Promise."

"Girls?" said Caroline.

"Slip of the tongue," said Kelsey.

He looked at them. Bookends. Arms folded, legs crossed, faces blank, watching him.

The Freeze.

"Come on," he said to the men—and then to the women, "be back in an hour."

They got up and moved toward their tents. "I think I've lost the love of two good women there, Alan," Kelsey said.

"I wouldn't even *joke* about that if I were you," he said. "You'd be dead or crazy inside of a month."

Kelsey laughed. Not far off the mark though, he thought.

"If it comes to that, no black limos, all right? And no New Orleans jazz bands either. Just a plain pine box and a vault at Scribner's. Where I'm wanted."

"You've got it."

Where I'm wanted, thought Walker. Damn it, Bernie. You don't have the foggiest notion, do you.

The trail was easy to follow and the four men moved quickly back through the scrub, up and then down the hill until the ravine was just below them and Graham could see the tall plants and the trap to one side where he'd left it.

"Okay," he said, "we're here. Everybody quiet now."

They moved carefully down into the gully, shotguns held out away from them, barrels up, only Graham without a gun, leading them, all of them silent but for the sibilant click of Graham's motor-driven camera—which he turned on Kelsey whenever he was sure enough of his footing to turn around. At the base of the hill they found the footpath and Graham did not turn at all then for fear of further traps.

They stopped to inspect the swatter.

"I remember something like this from Vietnam I think," said Kelsey, his voice very low. "Something like it."

They held their guns down now, stock to the armpit and barrel over the forearm. Then Ross took his in both hands in a ready position as Graham led them toward the marijuana.

"Here it is."

Ross looked up at it and whistled through his teeth. "That's something," he said.

"Sure is," said Kelsey.

Graham was taking photographs. Walker glanced around, looking for more traps. The heat was oppressive.

Ross plucked a twig from the nearest plant.

"I thought we weren't taking any," said Walker.

Ross grinned. "Just a little." Graham took his photo three times in rapid succession; the grin slid away.

"You've got to wonder who he is," said Kelsey.

"Who," said Ross, "the farmer? Some kid, probably."

Walker glanced back toward the trap. "Handy kid," he said.

"So he reads," said Ross.

The forest was very still.

"Hard to figure that it's a kid," said Kelsey.

"I'll tell you what I'd like to do," said Walker. "I'd like to get out of here."

"We saw it," said Kelsey, turning. "We can go."

They moved back across the trail to the swatter.

"I know that thing," said Kelsey, pointing at it. "I do. Vietnam or somewhere. I don't remember. Too much research over the years—clogs things up. But somewhere."

Halfway up the hill Alan Walker slipped on a patch of leaves.

He turned as he fell and found himself looking back the way they'd come, out over the gully—and as his eyelids fluttered with the impact of falling he thought he saw someone in the bushes a yard or two beyond the stand of marijuana looking out at the four of them clumsy and vulnerable climbing the hill, but then when he got up again there was nobody there and he thought it's nothing, just a flutter, just light on the leaves. They were alone.

CHAPTER FIFTEEN

It had happened strangely to him, because when first he saw them he knew they were hunters, campers, something like that, their clothes told it and the softness in the way they moved and walked, they were hunters or campers, civilians, and nothing to worry about; but then one of them had brought the shotgun up into combat position, and the point man began his slow, easy, measured walk, the guy on slack looking suddenly like he knew what he was doing, the guy at drag thin and prematurely white just like JD 2, their radioman, and Lee felt a fist grip his stomach that wouldn't let go, wouldn't stop—a cold nauseous wrench that clenched and twisted there. The dog was at full point, hackles raised. Lee watched them through the scrub, through blinding ashes and swells of heat. The sun in the trees angled spots of camouflage down over them.

They were and they weren't.

Cops civilians soldiers cong.

Whoever they were they'd found him.

One of them was using a camera. Another man tore a stem away. On the end of the stem were leaves and pods. His stem. His leaves, his pods.

So that mixed with the fear was anger now. At the touch of his fingertips on its neck the dog would attack. That option was there. A bolt was fitted into the crossbow already and the quiver attached to the stock held six more. If they were good he could kill two of them before they located his fire, the dog perhaps could get a third. If they weren't good he could kill them all and he wouldn't need the dog.

The trap was sprung. But he'd watched their approach and it hadn't been them, it was already sprung by then. That might mean there were more of them somewhere. Oddly enough the thought relaxed him a little, it took the edge off, the muscles of his arms drew out softer, because until he had the answer to that no confrontation was possible—and it was just too fast this way. Too fast. One moment he was alone and getting by just fine, thank you, he and the dog, preparing for just such a contingency because McCann had put a bee in his bonnet but not really believing it much and the next moment wondering how many men will die, how many men can he kill before it can all be made the same again. He wasn't ready.

There were things you had to do in order to keep yourself secure and they were given, exigencies of war, call in the napalm drop to destroy their cover even though it was basically just trees you were killing, wasting vast rich tracts of land, or sometimes torch a village that had been there a hundred years and was mostly women and children now but you had to do it because they might be able to use that too, or had been using it, or would use it again in the future—and these were things you did not really care to do but they made you more secure so you psyched yourself up and you took your time and did them. It saved lives, kept you out of a lot of firefights. It was easier if you had time to do it right so that civilians did not get hurt like they did in the little ville outside of Cu Chi that day, the ville that was not even supposed to be there, that was not on any maps, the one where they'd gone out looking for Ragweed and found him with his dick in his mouth out back of the hooches.

It was the VC under the floorboards in the dead whore's hooch that had started it, so goddamn sudden that they'd had no time to think but only to react so react they had—and look what that had caused.

Just look what that had caused.

You needed time if you could get it. To get things straight. Or sometimes they never got straight again.

No, the thing to do was to think this through, to use the brain the gray matter and work it carefully, then do what you had to do fast and well. The crops were his. This place was his. His territory, his cover. All he had. Every last fucking thing he had.

The thing to do was to follow them.

He watched them move back across the trail, past the Swing and up the hill. They moved well now. Steadily. Carefully. He couldn't figure them. Damn! He stood and stared as they angled upward. The pure fascination of the enemy—the first enemy clear out there in the daylight in a very long time. He saw the one who looked like JD 2 lose his footing, fall and turn in his direction. He dropped into the scrub.

Stupid! he thought. You stupid bastard! You could

have been seen. You might have been seen. From now on you keep your goddamn distance.

He waited. When the last of them crested the hill he started after them. They'd be visible again on the downward side. So he did not hurry.

"Heel," he whispered to the dog and the dog obeyed.

At the top he saw them in a grove of pine, moving down toward Basker's Pond. He was thinking they'd take the campsite there over on the western side. Good easy firebase that was. He cut off to the right where there was better cover and he wouldn't be seen, figuring to approach from the south. If he was wrong and they were elsewhere he could pick up their trail later.

Easy, he thought. No rush. You're on your own ground here. They're the strangers.

And then as he thought about them being strangers the one who looked like JD 2 did not look so much like him in his memory anymore despite the hair—he seemed more wiry and stringy than JD, hair still white but set over a craggy, golden face now, and the heavy one seemed shorter, stockier, face uglier and flatter, both men dressed in black, and the man with the camera looked more and more to him like some kind of sapper carrying another new trinket for the field with the body of a camera and all the guts removed, the guts replaced by a grenade, its handle held in the cocked position by the weight of the body as he set it on the ground so that all you had to do was come along and say, oh what's this what a great camera what a great pack of cigarettes what a great can of peaches or fruit cocktail and pick it up and that's your hands and face gone at least. Trust nothing. Trust no one. In the jungle the trees were sometimes triple canopy so that it was impossible to view the sun. Here they dappled you with light. It was still not possible to see clearly.

He walked toward the camp and the breeze was hot.

CHAPTER SIXTEEN

"So what do you say to some real hunting?" said Kelsey as they saw the camp ahead. "Birds for dinner."

"We've got no dogs," said Ross.

"We didn't need them last time," said Kelsey. He pointed east. "There's a clearing over there, just tall grass and a little scrub. Pheasant seem to love it. At least they used to. We managed to flush four or five without the dogs. Want to try it?" He looked at Walker.

Alan shook his head. "Maybe tomorrow, Bernie. One traipse through the woods is about my limit these days."

"Ross?"

"Sure, I'll go."

"How about you, Graham? Alan'll lend you his shotgun, right?"

Alan nodded.

Graham smiled at him. He was beginning to feel pretty comfortable with Kelsey. "Is this in the nature of a test?"

"A which?"

"A test. I was told there might be some testing.

132

Can he shoot, can he cast a fly rod. Can he handle climbing a mountain or two."

"My reputation's preceded me again."

"Afraid so."

"Hell, that's all TV interview stuff. *People* magazine. There's nothing to it. Besides, the way you mark a trail you already passed it."

They were coming into camp now. Caroline and Michelle had changed into bathing suits and lay side by side in lounge chairs, sunning themselves, Pepsi bottles beside them, Caroline in a skimpy green two-piece and Michelle in a one-piece of almost aerodynamic design, plunging up from the bottom over the hip to the waist and down over her breasts and back. Graham thought they both looked terrific, two sides to a very feminine coin.

"So what do you think?" he said.

"I'm wondering how you manage it," said Graham. And that was feeling pretty damn comfortable indeed.

"I meant the hunting."

"Right. Sorry. Sure, I'll go along. Only with just the camera. You know how it is. My dad was a hippie."

Kelsey turned to Walker. "There's a nice little stream up a ways. Not far. I was telling Caroline about it. It's sort of on our way. If you'd like to poke around awhile it's a good shady spot, and I think maybe you could get some company."

"Sounds fine."

Graham pointed the Nikon for some shots of the women. The magazine would not be opposed to a little celebrity skin especially under circumstances as odd

JACK KETCHUM

as these. As the men approached Michelle sat up and
slipped off her sunglasses. Graham was still shooting.
Kelsey started to walk past her to his tent and she
raised a strong tanned arm off the lounge chair. Kelsey
took her hand and gave it a squeeze, smiling at her. At
the corner of the frame Caroline turned toward them
and Graham photographed worry-lines etched mo-
mentarily into the mouth of that placid, aristocratic
face. Then it settled again.

My god, thought Graham, there are men who
would betray their best friend for either one of them
and Kelsey wants both.

Pride? Greed? Or did Kelsey really have a handle on
this? Maybe, thought Graham, he was one of the lucky
ones who knew precisely what they needed. The writing in *Double Veteran,* a long, cranky, rambling, and to
Graham's mind totally brilliant essay on women as vic-
tims and men as their victimizers, so scathingly personal regarding Kelsey's own sexual history as to make
you cringe sometimes, indicated to Graham that the
writer had meditated long and hard on the subject of
his needs and responsibilities, and what was often the
conflict between them. Not even those members of
the press who had attacked the book—and they were
legion—could deny that Kelsey took sex, in the broad-
est sense of the word, very seriously. So maybe he'd
given it enough thought that he knew what he was
doing. And maybe not. Maybe this was an attempt to
deny *in vivo* the more feminist-oriented critics' accusa-
tion that he was nothing more than a sexual throwback
to Hemingway and Henry Miller, trying to justify a life
of barely hidden misogyny.

If so, Kelsey was essentially frivolous—he was using these women. And they were smart enough so that sooner or later they'd see it. When they did they'd leave him.

There's no way to know, he thought.

You're only here for the duration.

Meantime, whatever happened, he was beginning to get the pictures, the documentation. There was no doubt in his mind that Graham was exploiting them. The pictures were for pay in a national magazine. They would be viewed one way if the trio stayed together, another way if they didn't. But there was also no doubt who he was rooting for. It was possible, he thought, to exploit people and care for them at the same time. Tricky but possible. Maybe even to love them.

And maybe love was like that anyway more or less, and maybe Kelsey knew it.

Outside the camp Lee watched the women dress, saw the men take up their guns again and then watched them all move out along the trail.

They were taking the trail.

Not smart, he thought. You could mine a trail. So why did I think they were good?

The women bothered him.

He didn't like to see the women there.

Alma.

No—that was bullshit. Everywhere in the world men had women, cops had wives too and pimps had whores, gangsters had whatever the hell gangsters had these days and soldiers had their camp follow-ers, *numba one GI go flik flik?* and you'd swab your poncho spread out on the cot with alcohol before and after and those same little girls who fucked you or cleaned your hooch would put ground glass in your drinks or razor blades in your apples or do like they did Ragweed.

It was good to remember they were dangerous too, the women.

He remembered the little mother in Saigon when he was on leave with Brown and JD 2. They were walking down the street looking for someplace to buy a pair of shoelaces when this woman came up to JD and said something, crying and panicky, and pointed into her baby carriage, backing off a little as she did so so that he knew something was wrong in there and it was not with her baby, but he guessed JD 2 didn't see it, because he only looked and parted the dirty linen, and Lee and Brown hit the street just before the charge took JD's face away. And they had shot that woman.

The other he remembered was just before the incident in the ville outside of Cu Chi. It had been weeks and weeks of patrols they were coming off of— weeks in the muck and rain, weeks and weeks of fear that the next field was the mine field and the sniper around the next corner and the trap just ahead on the trail, and every time something did happen there was never anybody around to shoot at, just spooks in the night, ghosts, coming out of ghostland and killing you and going, so that they were all wrung dry of everything but fear and frustration by the time the mine exploded under the brand-new cherry and they saw the little girl maybe twelve or thirteen years old half hidden in the bushes, her hand still on the detonator. They all had shot that one, shot her so many times you could see the chips of bones flying, chip by chip, the impact holding her up, standing, until everybody was empty.

And then there were more patrols after that. Two more weeks of them. And then the ville near Cu Chi. Then Sprinkles. To Lee it explained a few things, that sequence of events, it meant something, though it did not help things any.

The point, though, was about the women.

He waited till they were gone and then he and the dog walked into the camp. He looked down the hill to the pond to make sure they were all accounted for. Then he did an inventory.

Three cars. A Jeep, a Dodge wagon, and a Mercedes. Three tents, spaced close but not too close—that was good—all expensive and filled with clothes and gear. Supplies enough for three days, maybe four. His marijuana sitting on a flat stone to dry. Two axes and two hatchets, all new and sharp. A first aid kit, complete. Boxes of ammunition.

He took note of sleeping quarters. The women were in one tent and two men each shared the other two. He noted each tent's proximity to the fire. He inspected the pile of split wood and the kindling.

Judging from their gear, the setup of the camp, and the woodsmanship he observed he decided that somebody here knew something of what he was doing. They were probably mostly twinks but not all of them. The illusion he'd had earlier of quiet competence moving through the scrub was not, then, entirely unfounded. Why did he have to keep changing his mind about this? he wondered. He was out of practice. There was weakness there. He picked either the heavyset man or the younger skinny one as leader. One or both of them probably had most of the field knowledge. The others would be the reason they used the trail instead of going through the brush.

He thought he knew where they were heading.

He looked up and saw Pavlov by the embers of the fire. The dog had his right leg raised and was blithely pissing.

Why not? he thought. It's his damn territory. All this is.

When the dog was finished Lee snapped his fingers and the dog immediately heeled. They started off down the trail.

It would be necessary, he thought, to know more about them by nightfall.

He followed.

CHAPTER SEVENTEEN

"Mind if we stop here?" asked Michelle. She was eyeing a large flat rock that angled out into the stream. The men had gone on ahead.

"Fine," said Caroline. It was cool and shady.

"Mind if I inflict myself on you for a little while?"

"You going to make me feel guilty again?"

Michelle smiled. "Uh-huh."

"Go right ahead."

Caroline and Walker sat down under a tree a few feet from the stream. Michelle folded a beach towel over the surface of the rock. Then she stood up, planted her feet hip-distance apart, relaxed, and began her breathing. Soon she was moving her head in circles, relaxing her neck. They watched her go through the warmup. She was wearing baggy men's jeans and a loose blue cotton shirt over a thin white cotton bodysuit, leg warmers, and the lightweight hikers. Midway through the warmup she began discarding things. The shirt went first, then the boots and leg warmers, and finally, as she lay back on the rock for the heavy stomach and leg work, the jeans. By then her body was glistening.

Caroline watched with interest. Secretly, when

nobody was around, she'd been doing some of this herself. It was damn hard work and she hated it but at her age you had to do something.

She glanced at Walker. He was breaking off pieces of a twig and throwing them into the water. They eddied there. The shotgun lay beside him. His brow was furrowed slightly and he wasn't watching.

"Alan."

He looked at her. His effort at concealment was halfhearted. She'd seen him do much better.

"Suppose you tell me."

He looked at Michelle, close enough to hear.

Caroline laughed. "Good god, Alan. I'm already sharing the best stuff with Mich. I might as well share the shit as well."

He nodded, sighed, tossed the rest of the twig into the stream.

"It's the book, of course," he said. "I hate to say this. I don't know *how* to say it exactly except to be direct about it, so I will. The first two hundred pages are just no good, Caroline. They're rambling, disjointed. Frankly, they're boring. And somehow terribly *safe.* Safe. From Kelsey! There's no thrill, no flair. Hell, *Double Veteran* rambled. You know that. But it also had all the guts in the world.

"I don't know what's happening here, Caroline. There's nobody writing I admire more than Kelsey. But if this script just came across the transom I'd reject it. No way I can bring it to a publisher who's paid half a million for the thing. They'd want him to start all over again. And I mean that. Start from scratch. It's Scribner's for chrissake! They'd ask for a whole new book. And I hate to think what that could do to Kelsey's confidence. I really do. He took a bad beating on *Veteran*. But I only see one other alternative and he's not going to like that either."

"Another publisher."

"Right. I think we can go to Random House on this and they'd be willing to just dump this book on the market if we promise them the next two, and of course they'd buy out the contract for him. They've been after us for years now. He'd still have to cut, revise, but not start over again the way he would at Scribner's. I could make a pretty good deal with them too. The problem is it's Random House. Not Scribner's. And Kelsey'd have to finish a project the general consensus on which already is that it's not really worthy of him."

Caroline thought about it. She looked at Michelle. She was facing them, working on leg-lifts, listening.

"He could forget the book entirely, give Scribner's a new one."

"He could," said Walker. "Problem is he loses the movie deal that way, and that's another five hundred thousand dollars. Kelsey's not exactly money hungry, but . . . well, it's five hundred thousand dollars. And the hell of it is that the story, if he can just plow through and *get* to it, would probably make a pretty decent movie. It might just be successful."

"Damn. There's no good way, is there."

"Not that I can see. One way or another I've brought some bad news here."

"That's okay, Alan," she said smiling a little, "they no longer kill the messenger."

He shook his head. "I just don't understand. This book should have worked for him. It's a *romance,* on paper a thoroughly tough-minded romance. Different. The people are interesting, the situation's great. Hell, he's stolen all over the place from you and Michelle if you don't mind my saying so. He knows his subject. And it comes out . . . timid. Timid and confused. I don't get it. Is he drinking? Are you two . . ." He lowered his voice. ". . . is the marriage in trouble?"

"The answer to the first question is yes," said Michelle.

They looked at her. The white bodysuit was nearly transparent now. Lord, thought Caroline, she is beautiful.

"He's been drinking more. At least I think so. Caroline?"

"He has, yes. Though I've still never seen him drunk."

Michelle laughed. "Sure you have. He's just so damn good at managing it. But the answer to the second question, Alan, is no."

Caroline felt her cheeks flush and for a moment thought, How dare she.

"He may *think* it's in trouble," said Michelle. "In fact I'm sure he does. He wants us both and he's juggling, he's very aware of that, and I'm sure he feels bad about it in some ways, feels he's not giving either of us full measure. I think he feels guilty. Like he's built himself some kind of velvet trap here. It feels so good he never wants to leave it, never wants it to go away. But then he looks around at the rest of the world outside, at us, and what are we getting? He's got a con-

142

science so he feels guilty. For feeling so good. How can he be having this when the rest of the world can't? How can he be doing right by us two? And at the same time he's scared it will all go away. Will disintegrate. He feels he's living dangerously. When as far as I'm concerned he's not."

"No?" said Caroline.

"No. He loves you and he always will. At the same time he loves me. Deep down inside he knows there's room enough for both of us. There is. He's big. If I didn't know that I wouldn't be here. God knows I have no intention of competing with you. Kelsey gives me what I need, all of it, and no less. How about you?"

"The same I guess."

"You guess?"

"No. The same."

"Fine. Then it can last, can't it. He's not living dangerously at all. He just thinks he is."

They were silent for a moment. Walker looked a little dazed. Caroline realized that she'd literally been holding her breath.

That was some speech, she thought.

And she doubted there was a lie in it. Mich was honest the way few women were honest, and no men, the way she herself was not completely honest. So candid she had Alan blushing. The only flaw in it all might be what she thought she knew about Kelsey and didn't. What Kelsey himself might not know. She thought about the child Michelle was carrying and then about the abortion. Which might make all the difference in the world. If she let it.

"There's more to it," she said. "Bernie's not young anymore and he needs a book. Alan knows. Sales on *Veteran* weren't good. The reviews were downright criminal. Unfortunately he reads reviews. So who knows what he thinks? That he's been living on his reputation? That his powers are diminishing? And who knows, given what you say, Alan, maybe they are."

Walker shook his head. "No way. The essay on Cambodia we sold to *Harper's?* Brilliant, vintage stuff. A little longer and we could have published it as a book in its own right. No, it's this project or something. Maybe the drinking."

"I don't know, then. This macho crap—guns, prizefights, all-nighters with Ross and the rest—I get the feeling it's accelerating lately. And I think it's career stuff almost as much as it's worrying about Mich and me. The problem is he doesn't talk much anymore, so it's hard to say."

"He talks to me," said Michelle. "And you're right. It's both. I'm sure it is."

Hmmm, thought Caroline. *He talks to me.* Sometimes candor and a low blow were very hard to tell apart. The unconscious cruelty of the young.

"So then what we've got to do," Walker was saying, "is reassure him somehow. Me, that I can handle the business with the book one way or another and that he's as good as ever, basically. You, that he's not hanging by his teeth here."

Caroline sighed. "You know sometimes I get sick of it. I love the man. I'd probably kill for him. But sometimes you wish he were . . . ordinary, normal."

Michelle stood up, picked up her towel and stepped off the rock.

"If he were normal," she said, "you'd be bored to tears. You're not particularly ordinary and neither am I. We'd all just shrivel up and die."

"Hell, we'll do that anyway."

Michelle smiled. "Die, yes. Shrivel up, no. Not necessarily."

Caroline stood up too. "Speak for yourself," she said. "Remember that I'm way out here ahead of you."

They gathered up their things and moved downstream.

Kelsey was right, Ross thought, they'd already flushed one bird over by Graham but he guessed it was too far away for Kelsey because he hadn't fired, and his own shot had gone wide. Still it was early. They were crisscrossing the field right to left and then left to right, about fifty feet apart, moving slowly but erratically because it was the erratic pattern that confused the birds, scared them and got them up. Ross was in the middle now.

He looked at Graham, big kid's grin on his face and standing tall as possible, long lens pointed at Kelsey through the tall grass, his camera whirring. Dumbass kid. Getting photos of The Great Man hunting. Did anybody still buy that junk these days?

Hemingway was dead, wasn't he?

Well, he'd have to cut it soon now. The grass was getting higher as the field sloped down into a depression. It was up to his shoulders already. Tall thin yellow stuff that tickled his bare arms like stalks of wheat. Should have brought a hat, he thought. It was well into the afternoon but the sun was still fierce out here. Kelsey had a hat. I should have brought one.

He kept walking. He had to part the grass to see now.

Suddenly about thirty feet ahead of him he heard the quick roar of wings as the pheasant broke cover. A big one. He swung with the bird and slapped the trigger, heard Kelsey's new Citori like an aftershock of his own gun and saw the hit, his or Kelsey's, the bird flapping madly in an explosion of feathers. He fired again but this time he was wide. He saw the bird gain altitude for just a moment and then start to fall, fighting wildly to stay aloft. The echo of his shotgun rumbled through him.

He followed the fall. The sun on the grass in front of him gave the illusion of flatness, defeated his sense of distance. The bird drifted left, still alive, slapping the air, lurching, its sense of balance finished. He heard Kelsey's shotgun again and saw the bird lift abruptly with the impact, then plummet downward, and now he followed it carefully down into the wall of grass, wanting to be able to retrieve it, the bird falling nearest to him, knowing that Kelsey and Graham would also have trouble finding it, following it precisely down until it was almost into the high grass and then seeing something leap up suddenly to catch it in its jaws, a perfect interception, the big black muzzle of the shepherd locked perfectly into the pheasant's ruined breast, so distinct to him against the yellow grass that he could even make out the nick in the animal's ear.

"What the *fuck?*"

The grass ahead of him was still.

He looked at Kelsey, then at Graham. Both stood staring a moment. Then, together, they all began to move on the spot.

They stood there. Feathers. A little blood. And that was it.

"I thought we didn't *have* any dogs," said Ross.

"We don't," said Kelsey.

"Well somebody sure does."

"Somebody does," said Kelsey, "and the son of a bitch has got our dinner!"

They looked at one another, three amazed dumbstruck faces. Standing there impotently with their big-deal shotguns.

You had to laugh.

CHAPTER EIGHTEEN

Kelsey opened his eyes to a world of golden brown, of shimmering murk, in which bits of matter floated randomly—it was as though he were looking through a microscope without knowing what he was seeing there, some order beyond his range of understanding. He dove deeper.

The water held currents of warmth and chill and they played across his body. He was naked, unconfined, and the paunch felt lighter now, the legs stronger. He felt youthful, embraced by an atmosphere which challenged him, forced blood into his chest and shoulders as he pulled his arms to his sides and propelled himself forward. He felt pleasure, joy, almost a yearning, that this go on, that the lungs not force him up, that the blood stay hot, rushing. He pushed up, out and back with his arms again, scissored his legs, and the water turned black beneath him.

His buoyancy pulled at him. He released a measured breath and it subsided. He drifted deeper. But now his lungs began to ache. One last dive, he thought. It was black, black—his eyes were open, pupils dilated, but he couldn't even see his arms as he raised them and began to push downward. Black as death down there. The water colder. He kicked, felt pressure in his ears, in his chest, drew up his arms again and finally, gratefully, touched bottom. It was soft—repulsive in a way yet cool and strangely lovely, the feel of smooth thin clay, of slime that was almost like silk, of silk that was like corruption. He grasped it, squeezed it, felt it melt and bleed in his hands. And now his lungs were hammering him.

He turned and pulled himself up, hand over hand, as though climbing some great invisible ladder, arms and legs aching too now, thick, solid, engorged with blood. There was a brown-green bowl of light above him. He climbed and watched the sunlight flicker and the living, floating things drift by, whirling in the eddy of his climb.

He broke the surface, gasping.

"Jesus fucking *Christ,* Kelsey!"

It was Michelle, four feet away and wiping water from her eyes—she too had just surfaced.

"I've been down there *looking* for you! You ass-hole! Don't *do* that to me!"

He gasped again and said he was sorry.

"I touched bottom, though."

"You what?"

"I touched bottom."

She looked at him and shook her head.

"You're a child."

She swam closer, sputtering, her face softened now. They treaded water there.

"What was it like?"

"Clay. Soft. I liked it."

He smiled at the look in her eyes.

"Swim in with me a little," she said. "Closer to shore. Where we can stand."

He followed her. He saw Ross and Graham off to one side standing in the water, talking, Graham moving his arms back and forth lazily across the surface. The sun was low on the horizon. Ross was speaking. They were too far away to hear. He straightened up. His toes could just touch now. It was grittier, sandier here.

He half bounced, half swam toward her. She turned and he could see her breasts naked in the water.

"You too?"

"It was your idea."

"Yeah, but I didn't think you bought it."

She shrugged and came toward him. Her hands found his hips.

"Why not?"

"You're modest."

"Am I?"

"Sure you are."

"I was practically naked in front of Alan and Caroline today."

"The white suit?"

"The white suit."

"I take it back, then."

She reached around in front of him and smiled. Her touch was electric.

"I'm not modest. Not at all."

He drew her toward him. He saw her glance at Ross and Graham, then back to him. She put one leg over his hip and guided him slowly into her, the shock of her warmth gripping him, making him tremble. She brought up the other leg and locked her ankles behind him, put her arms around his neck. He took the strong cool buttocks in his hands and rocked her gently over him. Heat and then liquid cool. Heat and cool. He looked into her eyes, saw the pleasure there, and knew she saw his own. Beside them the water barely rippled.

"So you touched bottom," she said.

"I did."

"Was it like this? Soft like this?"

"Nothing is like this."

"Nothing?"

"Nothing."

"I love to feel you inside me. Why is it still so good, Kelsey?"

"I don't know. It shouldn't be. A year now. More."

"We should be bored with one another."

"Bored. Looking elsewhere."

"I want to suck your cock. I want you in my mouth."

"Can't. With all of them around."

"I know."

"You feel deprived?"

"Yes."

"Yes?"

"Not really."

"Sure?"

"I'm sure."

"I want you to want to."

"I do. I do want to."

"Good."

"I always want to."

"Good. Thank god."

From above Caroline watched Kelsey leave the water and lie down on his belly in the late afternoon sunlight, his body glistening, his shadow long, disappearing beside him into the foliage. Michelle was swimming laps across the width of the pond—precise, graceful strokes, evenly paced. She could see that like Kelsey, Mich was naked and thought, if I were a man I'd want her. Graham and Ross said something to one another and then began swimming after her. She could see that they were naked too. Graham did a lot of splashing.

She turned and went back to Walker. They'd put paper and kindling down for the cooking fire together and now she saw that Alan had stacked the logs, had already lit one side and was striking a match to light the other. Smoke billowed up from the paper. Flames rose hungrily. The kindling began to crackle.

They stepped away from the sudden heat.

"I think I'd like a drink," she said.

Walker grinned. "Thought you'd never ask."

"There's some Stoli there in the ice chest. The red one."

"Fine. Straight up for you?"

"Please."

He got the drinks and handed her her glass. They stood by the fire, fascinated.

"Thanks."

"Cheers."

"Cheers."

Dusk was falling. The vodka was ice cold. It slid down like fiery syrup.

I wonder what he really thinks of us, she thought. He's not a judgmental person but I wouldn't be surprised if he thinks I'm crazy. For not overtly fighting this one. He's seen the others but he knows that this one's different. I wonder what he thinks. I wish he were one to say. I wonder what he'd say if he knew that she's pregnant—and then knew what I've considered doing about it. In his quiet way he's a fighter. I've seen him slug it out for contracts and I saw him fight Jocelyn's cancer. Still I think he'd hate me. I think maybe I'd hate myself.

Maybe.

"He'll be all right," said Walker. She guessed he'd been watching her. "Don't worry."

"You think so?"

"I definitely think so. There's just a lot on his mind right now. Something he's going through. It'll end."

"Prove it."

"Eh?"

"Prove it will end. Tell me how."

"I can't. I just know."

"Faith, Alan? You? Really?"

He laughed. "Something like that. Not exactly."

She finished her drink. So did Alan. He poured her another.

"I guess I'd better get to it, though," he said. "I'll talk with him tonight, if that's all right with you. Give him the next two days to think about it without actually being able to *do* something."

"A grace period."

"Yes."

"That sounds right."

They sipped their drinks and watched the fire.

"There's nothing else, Caroline? Nothing I don't know about that might also be . . . affecting him?"

"Not that I'm aware of. Ask Mich. He talks to her. Remember?"

Alan smiled. "I knew the claws were there somewhere."

"Oh, they're there all right. I just keep them nicely trimmed, that's all. She's arrogant as hell sometimes but I happen to like her. Damn it."

"She reminds me a little of you sometimes."

"Oh sure. Me and my blonde muscles."

"No. You and your wicked mouth. Remember when you called me a damn bloody carpetbagger on the Nixon book?"

"I was offended."

"You were right. And I caught hell for it too. Then the thing died on me anyway. And I thought I was being so smart."

"We were younger then."

"A little, yes. We were."

"A lot."

Michelle walked up the hill and saw them by the fire. She was wrapped in a towel now and carried a pair of sandals. She was scowling. Mad. She walked up to Caroline and stood there rigid and then she shook her head.

"I'll tell you something, Caroline," she said. "I wouldn't say this to Kelsey because god knows what would happen and it's our first day out here. But if that little prick Charles Martin Ross lays so much as a finger on me again I'm going to deck him. I'm going to knock his ass right down into his kneesocks."

They stared at her. And they must have looked pretty funny too because her anger broke right there and she started laughing.

"I mean it!" she said, giggling. "This is serious!"

"Gee. Should we ask what happened?"

"No. Don't bother. Let's just say that the jerk seems to think he's a tit man. He isn't."

And then they all laughed.

"You guys," said Michelle, still laughing, walking toward her tent. "You guys go ahead. Go ahead! But I'm telling you, I'll cut his little pooter off. I will!"

They cracked up.

Just the girl to do it, too, thought Caroline.

She disappeared into the tent, and she and Walker were still rolling—and god! It felt good!

Inside the tent the air was close, steamy with moist heat trapped all day in there. As soon as she finished she'd open the flaps, get some circulation. The tent still had a new store-bought smell to it that wasn't entirely pleasant. She was sensitive to smells. Her hair now, her body—those were good smells.

At the pond she'd used some of Kelsey's expensive no-phosphate shampoo and the biodegradable soap and had herself a bath. Unless you went deep or else out to the more stagnant middle of the pond the water was clean enough. She'd needed a bath after the workout, the diving, the sex and the swimming, and then needed it even more after Ross had put his hands on her. Now she toweled dry.

Men like Ross repelled her. He reminded her of a photographer she'd known back in the early starving days when she needed every job she could get—this guy took every possible opportunity to adjust you, touch you, brush up against an arm or a leg or a thigh. A completely obvious creep. She needed the work so she'd sat still for it through the shoot but then promptly called her booker. It was the last they'd sent her there. She'd heard recently that he wasn't working anymore. It was inevitable. In fashion photography that type didn't last long. They went on to the stroke mags or to shooting people's kids and weddings. But in the real world they were everywhere. Waiters, cabbies, construction workers on the corner. Men like Kelsey and Walker, men who respected a woman's dignity, were the exception not the rule. The rule was furtive. It sniggered and brushed your ass as you passed by.

She dug into her bag for a stick of Gatorade gum, opened it and popped it into her mouth. She pulled on a pair of panties, a clean pair of jeans and a fresh shirt. She sat down and put on polo socks and a pair of runners. Then she dug into the bag again for her hairbrush, found a ChapStick first and used it, and then found the brush. She stood up and started brushing.

And heard something hit the tent.

It was heavy and it made her jump.

What the hell? she thought.

Ross? Getting even?

It had hit the left side of the tent, the side nearest the woods. She stepped to the tent flap and opened it.

Ahead of her Walker and Caroline were still sitting by the fire, still talking, and now she saw Kelsey, Graham, and Ross coming up the path from the pond. It wasn't Ross, then.

She was about to step outside when something made her look down. And made her jump again.

Gliding around the corner toward the raised lip of the tent was the biggest blacksnake she'd ever seen.

She threw the tent flap closed and zipped it shut.

She took one deep breath and then another. Then she thought. Okay, there's a snake out there and you don't like snakes one bit. Okay. You can call Kelsey. He doesn't like them either but you can call him. Or you can wait for it to go away. Of course that might take a while.

Or you can kill the sonovabitch.

Where is it? she thought. They hadn't used it yet. Where the hell was it?

She moved her bag and then the nearly empty backpack and found it over in the corner—the hatchet Kelsey had suggested they keep there. Just in case. Well, this was definitely in-case. She picked it up and unzipped the tent flap. She parted it carefully and peered outside.

Nature, she thought, Jesus Christ.

The snake stuck its wide black head over the lip of the tent and began to crawl inside.

She stepped back.

Oh shit.

The head was down now into the tent, the tongue going, black eyes gleaming. It moved steadily, fast.

She stepped to one side.

I just hope it doesn't rain, she thought, and brought the hatchet down through the snake behind the head and down through the tent as well, down deep into the dirt.

The snake's jaws opened and closed, opened and closed. The body writhed.

Michelle skittered past it, outside.

Kelsey was looking at her strangely.

She walked toward him, still holding tight to the hatchet.

"What is this," she said, "the Garden of Eden?"

Her voice was probably a little shaky. So that all of them looked at her now.

"Either somebody just tossed a snake at me or one fell out of a tree. Do snakes climb trees? Well this one did. The biggest, blackest thing I ever saw. I killed it. I also killed the tent. And I am *not* cleaning up. Anybody care to see?"

"Hell, yes," said Kelsey. He took the hatchet away from her.

She really didn't mind at all.

Lee watched them from the brush.

He'd learned a few things.

The men were not bad with their weapons. They were not particularly great with them either but he'd have to be careful.

The dog hadn't spooked them. Nor had they worried about an owner possibly being nearby. So they did not feel in any danger. Perhaps it was their firepower, maybe their number. He'd seen it before. You got lucky for a while so you got complacent. So complacent that before too long a single man could walk right 'round your camp at night and turn every claymore inward so that when they fired, they fired right at you, right in your faces, not at the enemy. Your own mines killed you.

Then he'd tossed the snake and the woman had acted well and promptly. Okay. He would not underestimate her.

He slid off into the brush, back a few yards to where the dog waited.

It was dusk.

Tonight, he thought. A little later.

To use the complacency. To have most of them sleeping. To do it the old way, under the stars.

He felt filled with a burning manic energy and younger than he had in years. The heaviness of the past few days was gone. Stay gone, he thought. Fuck off. I'm doing something now. Take a hike.

He felt almost like whistling. Later there would be wariness, danger, maybe even terror. Now there was the excitement of knowing what was coming and knowing in your gut what you were here to do.

Circling wide around them he started toward his own camp.

"I love you, dog," he whispered. He reached down and patted his head. "You hear that, buddy? Do you?"

The dog heard him.

CHAPTER NINETEEN

"You did *what?*"

Kelsey looked at Ross as though he'd just swallowed a piece of sour, gone-over meat.

Oh you really *are* a nasty little prick, thought Caroline.

Ross stared back in all innocence. Ross would, she thought. He looked at Walker and then at Graham for support and got none of it—Walker, in fact, looked ready to wring his neck. Graham just watched him, neutral. He didn't even bother with the women—and that at least was smart.

It was a farce but Ross seemed ready to play it out.

"Jesus, Bernie. I was just trying to build up a little steam here. I told him I knew for a fact that you had about two hundred pages now and that he'd probably be seeing them soon. That's all. What's the big deal? Hell, he was real excited."

"I'll bet he was," said Walker, glaring. "Excited enough to read your play, I'll bet."

Ross didn't answer.

"You had no goddamn right," said Kelsey.

Caroline collected the last of the dinner plates, set

them down by the pots and pans beside her, and sat down by the fire between Michelle and Walker, opposite Kelsey. Tell him, she thought. Tell the little weasel.

Instead, Walker did.

"Look, I don't know who the hell you think you are but I'm Bernie's agent. If anybody comes to Bernie's editor with information about a project—anybody— it's either Bernie or I. Not you. Not you, dammit. Never. Not even Caroline would dream of doing such a thing and she's his wife. It's not your news to announce. You just don't do that and you damn well know it."

"Alan, it was just a piece of lunchtime conversation."

"Bullshit! Why in the world Bernie would even mention it to you is completely beyond my comprehension and staggeringly naive in my opinion but since he did you were expected to treat it in confidence. You didn't."

Ross turned to Kelsey again, insulted now.

"Did you say that? Did you tell me that this was in confidence? Did you *ever?*"

She felt a flash of anger at Kelsey. Why in the hell did he look so damned *disappointed!* He knew what Ross was.

Please, a little anger here.

"Did I have to?" said Kelsey.

"Yes! If you didn't want me to tell him, yes!"

"Ross, you knew I was having trouble with the book."

"I didn't *say* anything to him about that. God,

what do you take me for? Hell, I'd never tell him that."

"Wonderful. Thank you."

Ross looked at Graham for help again. Graham just shrugged and looked away into the fire.

"Fuck you, Ross," said Michelle.

Her voice was soft and all the worse for that. As though Ross weren't worth shouting at.

It was immediately as though a wall had appeared between them, or a series of walls that separated Ross from the rest—Walker's, Michelle's and her own were one, made of naked anger; Graham's was embarrassment and noninvolvement. Kelsey's alone was made of softer stuff, of sadness and weariness and disappointment. Still each served to isolate him. She felt it and Ross felt it.

"Who needs this shit," he said. He stood. "I was trying to do you a favor."

He walked away toward the pond.

Mich watched him go and then shook her head. "Sure you were," she said.

Bernie turned to Walker. "So. Now what?"

"I think we need to talk," said Walker.

Caroline grabbed a stack of plates.

"Come on, you two," she said. "Help me with the dishes."

They stood up and Graham collected the pots while Michelle went to the Jeep for soap and sponges. Caroline watched Kelsey pour himself a scotch. You'll need it, she thought. She caught Walker's eye. I can handle it—that was what the look said. But Kelsey seemed tired to her. Her anger toward him was gone though his response still disturbed her. He wasn't hard and probably never would be. It was a fault in one way and then again it wasn't.

"Ready?" she said.

Michelle seemed to hesitate.

"What."

"Ross," said Michelle.

"Oh, to hell with Ross," she said. "Come on."

"Listen. Would you mind very much if I left it to you two? I should do a few things anyway. Work out a little. I won't be in the way."

"Fine with me. Alan?"

"Fine."

Mich handed her the sponges and soap.

"Wait a minute," said Graham. "We need something." He went into his tent and came out with a three-cell flashlight, the kind you could focus up from spot to flood.

"Work lights," he said.

"Good."

Michelle stayed in the shadows by the road, lightly working, just stretching mostly, trying not to watch the men by the fire.

Things looked grim. Kelsey was drinking steadily and though Walker was not he was apparently not going to stop him. She saw him run a hand through his hair and then look at Walker intently as though trying to figure something out. She saw him pour another drink. Then toss a twig onto the fire and say something to Alan, opening his arms wide as if to say, what can I do? what can I say? and she hated to see it.

Confusion and doubt always made you smaller, she thought, at least while they had you. She knew it would pass and that his strength would return. She believed that out of all her knowledge of him. But she also knew you never returned to square one. You took the blows and came back either a little bit better or a little bit worse than before but not the same. And she'd liked him fine the way he was. The man she'd met backstage on that awful TV talk show who was so very nervous and funny in the dressing room while she was so deathly calm; and then, when they went out there, the situations were reversed and *she* was the one who was terrified, chattering away like an idiot while he was so easy in the face of those moments that counted, so in command of it all that he'd made it easy for her too, she'd felt like somebody who was dancing with Astaire—you couldn't make a wrong move. And afterwards he'd said, I would give my socks to sleep with a woman who comes back as good as you do and she'd said, hand them over. She'd never regretted it. She was restoring an Arizona ranch house for them and she'd wanted the same man there she'd begun construction for. She wouldn't get that now. She'd get somebody better or somebody worse and though either one would do, she could love either of them, she still had her fingers crossed.

She shifted the leg-extension to work the left side and looked up. She saw them deep in conversation.

Dammit, she thought, I'm not concentrating. This is very good way to get hurt here. Quit it.

She straightened up. Despite the breeze she was sweating. One more set, she thought. Concentrate.

"Hey!" It was Graham's voice, coming from the pond.

She saw Walker and Kelsey stand by the fire. Kelsey waved her over. She guessed that for now at least they were finished talking. She wrapped the towel around her neck and walked over.

"What's up?"

"Don't know," said Kelsey.

He seemed okay. She wondered what they'd resolved. If anything.

"You going down?"

"Sure. You never know with Graham."

"One minute. Let me get something on my feet."

She went to the tent and slipped on a pair of sneakers and they started down.

"Give us some light here."

Why were they in darkness? thought Kelsey. He'd seen Graham pick up the flashlight.

"Give us some light, will you?"

Then it was on them. The flood beam. They stepped down carefully. He could see Graham grinning and Ross and Caroline with their backs to him, looking down into the pond.

Graham played the beam across the water for a moment.

Kelsey looked up and thought he saw a pair of eyes glinting in the trees, somewhere over on the far shore.

Raccoon, he thought.

He looked again. It was gone.

The beam came back to them and they finished the

climb. They were standing on a narrow lip of sand between the hill and the pond where they'd spread their towels earlier.

"Just stand here a moment," said Graham.

He doused the light.

"Wait."

There were stars but no moon. It was very dark.

Caroline stood directly in front of him. Michelle was by his side.

He thought about the book. Alan had given him the options. He could dump it and the movie deal that went with it, or he could switch houses, or else he could start over, restructure the thing. Of course that last one was a little awkward now that Ross had opened his mouth to Samuels, his editor.

He didn't want to think about Ross. The debt was still there but he couldn't pay it this way, not if Ross was going to do his own collecting. And with malice. He suspected this would have to be the end of him and Ross. It was too damn bad because he remembered the boy in the man and the boy wasn't half bad. He remembered better times, things shared. It had been there. Before bad faith had become a question between them. But now for everybody's sake he supposed he had to say enough.

And he was not too good at good-byes.

Damn! He kept coming back to the book. He'd known it was off target but not this far. Where was his judgment? He was forty-three years old—a writer half his life. He was supposed to know something. He was supposed to be a pro for god's sake.

It tied in to Ross. Maybe even to the women.

What else was he fucking up here?

Beside him Mich shifted in the dark.

"Okay," said Graham. "Watch now." He turned on the light and adjusted its focus to a single narrow spot. He trained it on the water about six feet ahead of them and held it there. The water was the color of amber under the spot. They could see bottom. Tiny bits of matter hung suspended like particles of dust, drifting. As Kelsey watched their number seemed to increase gradually and a moment later he realized that they were alive, he saw movement, a slow swirling motion, and the water seemed to thicken until he became aware that there were other, slightly larger creatures in there now, all drawn to the light and to one another. Predators and prey. Thousands of them. An entire ecosystem down there—tiny, rich, growing. He thought of mayfly nymphs and larvae. A full swarm now, dizzying and thick as a sandstorm and all of them feeding. Feeding.

"My god," said Michelle.

He saw beetles, gigantic in comparison with the others, immense. Water striders rode the surface tension, casting shadows along the bottom.

Feeding.

"Watch," said Graham. He widened the beam.

The first frog seemed to appear out of nowhere at the outer rim of light. The second came up under it. A water strider disappeared. Then another. Two, three, then four more heads broke water. Still the swarm beneath them increased in size and density.

Then the frogs started scattering.

The pond's dominant life-form was making its appearance.

Leeches.

Lots of them, coming in from every angle and moving with elegant grace, stretching and retracting, large and long and then stubby-small again, looping into the light in a swift forward glide, their black backs studded with a brilliant red and yellow, snaking through the water. They were beautiful in a way, he thought, fascinating even as they revolted him. He heard Caroline gasp, saw the leech hit the frog like a torpedo so that it leapt out of the water and then disappeared beyond the circle of light.

He saw another frog snatch a beetle.

The dance of death continued.

"You realize?" said Ross. "We *swam* in that soup today."

"It's pretty much harmless in the daylight," said Kelsey. "You're drawing all the leeches out now because sight is just about the only sense they've got and we're the only game in town. During the day they're spread throughout the pond—especially, I guess, over on the deeper, stagnant side. You might want to stay away from that tomorrow."

"But you notice? No fish. None. That's what you get when you tinker, when you stock trout in a pond that nature made for bass."

"I guess it belongs to them now," said Michelle. "To the leeches."

"Unless the bass come back," said Ross.

"They won't come back," said Kelsey. "They

haven't in the years since I've been here, so I think it's fair to say they've had it. We fucked up, that's all. Everything's all out of whack now. We didn't think. We tinkered."

Graham drew the beam off the water. "Ready?"

"Sure," said Kelsey.

The flashlight swept the distant shore again but Kelsey saw nothing this time where the eyes had been.

Raccoon? he wondered. That thieving dog? There was even supposed to be a bear or two up here now and again. Whatever it was it was no doubt far away now.

Graham opened the beam to flood and they started up the hill.

The night was cooler, comfortable, and Kelsey thought that he could sleep. A little oblivion for a while. It would be good not to have to think for a few hours. It was what he'd come here for, basically, and instead the book had followed him and now there was Ross to consider too—and there was always Mich and Caroline.

He would have liked a little diversion, but the only diversion was the pond and they'd seen that, so he guessed that sleep would do.

CHAPTER TWENTY

He did not sleep.

The others had gone to bed hours ago—all but him and Graham. They sat by the fire working on a bottle of scotch. They were not precisely drunk but Kelsey was glad not to be going anywhere.

They hadn't said all that much of any import and it was a relief. Graham did not ask questions, did not try to pump him, and it reinforced Kelsey's impression that he was probably a pretty decent guy as magazine people went. He was also a fan. And that was nice because he also had the notion that Graham was widely read. Unusual for a photographer.

He passed the bottle and fed a few twigs into the fire.

They'd been talking about Seattle and then New York, which Kelsey loved and Graham didn't, and then about muggers and muggings because Graham had been robbed once in the East Village years ago and Kelsey had asked him, did he know where the word came from, *mugger*. Graham said no. So Kelsey explained about the British Romanies, the gypsies who made pots and mugs to sell and were also associated, however accurately, with assault and theft. From there they got onto word origins and peculiar turns of phrase.

"Words can make you lazy," said Kelsey. "You get used to them so they encourage sloppy thinking—or no thinking at all. I remember Bucky Fuller used to complain about how we were all still saying that the sun went down when we'd already had about three hundred years since Galileo to get used to the idea that it didn't.

"We talk about building a fire. Making a fire. Building, making—those are constructive words, creative words. Right? When what fire is about is destruction. Fire is a breaking down. You see?"

He fed another branch into the center of the flames. They watched the bark burst and peel away.

"Hell, it's our single best discovery. Forget the wheel. Forget the plough. It's fire. It keeps us hairless types warm, cooks the food for our delicate stomachs, provides light at night to make up for our puny eyesight. Easily our best discovery. The secret of how to break life down, of how to destroy matter. Look at it. It's wild. Incredibly destructive. Every animal but man is scared to death of it, terrified of these little explosions we make in the atmosphere. Even we were, once. But nights like these, out here, for thousands of years we've used it to protect us. And it *does* protect us. But it also separates us from every other living creature.

"Kind of a dilemma, don't you think? We know only the secret of death, not life. Fire. That's what we have to protect us, but it makes us *de facto* the enemy.

We smoke cigarettes, pipes, marijuana! We *stink* of fire. Do you realize how fierce that is? No wonder they avoid us. No wonder we're isolated. So you sort of have to ask, how do we get to know about *life* in that case, as a species, from the outside looking in?"

Graham shrugged. "I don't know. From one another?"

"From a man? Another human? Can you see your own eyes?"

"Sure—in a mirror."

"Ah, yes, but they're backwards."

They laughed. Graham had just swallowed. Kelsey saw the scotch claw at his throat. He coughed.

"Damned hard thing to see yourself," said Kelsey. "You take death. Your own dying. Ever give that much attention?"

Graham shook his head. "I've got a will."

"Other than that?"

"No. Not really."

Kelsey drank again.

"I kill a character in a book, I've got to think about dying. Really seriously entertain the thing. If it's fast and bloody, something like *Response to Impact,* I've got to feel the temperature of the blood, I've got to taste it in my mouth. Blood tastes salty but there's a sweetness to it. Blood sugar, right? It's real. I've tasted it here in my head till it's turned my stomach. Or if it's a quiet death I've got to hear the heart stop. The flesh has to waste away, maybe, the muscle tone has to go, the organs wither. It's got to be *me* dying. Me."

"Personally I like photography. You take your shot and walk away."

"That's right. There's no self-pity in this, don't get me wrong—but I never quite get to do that. I never quite get to walk away."

He tossed a length of pine onto the fire.

"It's a damn strange way to make a living."

"Good perks, though," said Graham, holding up the bottle, pulling on the expensive single-malt whiskey.

"Oh yes," laughed Kelsey. "Good perks all right."

In her tent Michelle was still awake. She could hear the men laughing by the fire.

It was hard to lie there, wanting him. She'd always had trouble the first night, sleeping in a new place. No matter where it was. There had been many new places lately and it was always the same. On an assignment she would go to bed at six just so she could fall asleep by ten and be rested enough for the morning shoot.

And now it would have helped to have him there.

She turned in the sleeping bag and closed her eyes. Then she opened them again. Caroline was looking at her, firelight in her eyes. It was as though she'd read her mind.

"You could go to him, you know it doesn't bother me."

"You're awake."

"Uh-huh. I meant it. You could if you want."

They were just a foot apart but it was almost impossible to see. Some vague shape in the darkness, facing her.

"No."

"Why not?"

Good question, she thought.

"I wouldn't do that."

"Why not?"

"I just wouldn't."

Silence then. Both of them just lying there. She could hear Caroline breathing. She could almost hear their two brains humming a little short of alpha.

She laughed. "I don't understand you, Caroline," she said.

"What's to understand?"

"You're not jealous. Sexually jealous. Not as far as I can see. I can't quite wrap around it. I would be."

"You're not me."

"No offense but I wouldn't want to be."

"Ouch!"

"That came out wrong. I'm sorry, honestly. It's just that, to me, it seems to mean you don't care about him. Not . . . enough. Not completely."

"Of course I care."

"Then why . . ."

"Look. I have seen more psychiatrists than you have muscles. I'm peculiar. Sexually I'm peculiar. But I'm also brighter than every shrink I've ever met and so they don't tend to help much.

"I grew up a certain way. Low self-esteem they tell me. Daddy was a perfectionist and I just wasn't perfect. Of course to be perfect I'd have had to have been born a boy, and I wasn't. But to make a long story short, I got rejected a lot, first by him and then, because I was an awkward kid, by most of the boys I wanted. No, by *all* the boys I wanted. That's the problem with good taste and standards. Then I discovered sex. I found out that if you fucked a boy he tended to come back for more. Any boy. So I fucked a lot of boys. And they hung around.

"But that still left me with this self-esteem problem. I couldn't . . . let go. I couldn't give anything, I didn't *have* anything, I wasn't worth anything. I *never* had an orgasm. Not once. See, I was fooling these guys. I didn't deserve them. Then when I was twenty-two I met this one guy I did deserve and you guessed it, he was a total prick—handsome, empty, and stupid, with a nasty streak in him, too, and wouldn't you know it, I had orgasms all day long.

"So that's where I was when I was twenty-two and that's still basically where I am today. Oh, I understand the problem but understanding doesn't always help despite what the shrinks say. It takes a good selfish nasty little bastard to get me going.

"Love just doesn't do it.

"What's changed is that I refuse to be bothered anymore with nasty little bastards. Why degrade yourself? So I pass on sexuality. Kelsey gives me love that isn't sexual and believe me, I've found over the years that with respect in your job and respect and love from a man, you can live on that just fine. You can *thrive.*"

Michelle thought about it.

"Bastards, huh?"

"Bastards."

They lay in silence.

"You must *love* Ross," said Michelle.

"Not even god loves Ross," said Caroline.

Then both of them were laughing.

By the time Kelsey went to bed they'd finished the bottle of scotch and Graham, who was unused to such nights, sat alone by the fire feeding it slowly as Kelsey had done and drinking bottled water. Being drunk was about ninety percent dehydration and he knew the dangers of going to sleep in that condition. He found some aspirin in the first aid kit and tossed back three of them against the other ten percent and then started seriously on the water.

It had been a good day, he thought. He'd gotten some good pictures, especially while they were hunting and then, toward dusk, around the campsite. Still you couldn't afford to waste the morning on a hangover. Kelsey was an early riser and he wanted to be ready.

He grinned. You silly bastard, he thought. Getting ripped with a subject. And he was ripped. Very. The fire, the whole damn campsite had a tendency to drift slightly. But it had been impossible to resist—hell, it was Kelsey. How often was a guy like that going to get smashed with you?

You took it when you got it.

He was tired. Ross would be long asleep in the tent they shared together. You should be too, he thought.

He stared into the fire. The fire drifted left this time. Graham focused. With difficulty.

A wind was coming up. He could feel it ruffle his hair. But the night was still mild and comfortable. He looked up and the sky was cloudless, blue-black, filled with stars.

He would have liked to sit up till dawn, he thought. Once, on a night like this, he'd made camp in a grove of birch trees and sat alone there till the sky lost its color, went completely black but for the stars, and then listened while the night sounds faded, ceased, all the crickets and frogs. It was windless that night and for a moment before the birds began singing the forest was so absolutely still that he imagined he could hear the leaves above him opening to the first, as-yet-unseen rays of the sun. Hundreds, thousands of leaves—the aspirant rustle of tiny clenched fists opening to the sky. He looked up and could see nothing. But he would still swear that he heard it to this day, a gentle breathing sound like distant breakers.

Was I drunk that night? he thought.

No, I was smoking pot.

He thought of what Kelsey'd said—*we stink of fire*.

They'd stolen some today. It wasn't dry yet. Tomorrow maybe.

He closed his eyes and opened them and the fire was drifting again.

Got to stop the drifting, he thought. Sit here till I do.

He reached for the water.

He heard nothing, nothing at all as the man came around behind him and looped the length of wire over his head and around his neck and twisted, pulling up and back, hard and abruptly, his knee in the small of Graham's back, tightening the wire so that the larynx cracked, the flesh parted, and the artery burst, blood sizzling into the campfire.

His head pointed toward the stars. It was finished quickly.

His sight went last.

CHAPTER TWENTY-ONE

He lifted the man to his shoulder and carried him into the brush. Then he went back to the fire. He piled on more logs so that the bloody ones would be sure to burn. He turned one of the stones. Using his knife he scraped the dirt up where the man had bled, turned it and then stepped on it carefully to pack it down. He capped the man's water bottle and put it back with the others.

He walked to the tent he knew to be the dead man's and peered inside. The fatigues, the nightfighter cosmetics made him feel like a ghost. The other man was sleeping. It would not be possible to kill him and still assure utter silence in such narrow confines as the tent—not with all their gear in there and there were other things to do. He waited for his eyes to adjust to the deeper darkness, breathing shallowly through his mouth, and froze there.

Five minutes later he was able to make out the carrying case for the photo equipment and as soon as he did he went inside. The sleeping bag was open. He pulled it apart and rumpled it slightly so it would look as though it had been slept in. He reached for the strap on the camera and drew it out through the tent flap. He set it beside the man's body in the brush.

Then he went to the Jeep.

There was still an hour left till dawn when he was finished. He hoisted the corpse onto his shoulder again, picked up the camera case and walked off into the brush. The body was more rigid now and hard to carry. A few yards down the line the dog was waiting.

They worked their way through the scrub down and around to the far side of the pond where it was deepest and he set the body down. He stripped it and set the clothes aside. As usual the man had evacuated his bladder and bowels as he died. The dog sniffed at him with interest. He wrapped the strap of the camera bag around the man's neck, tied it securely, opened it and emptied out film and lenses. In the interstices between the Nikon and the Rolie he shoved as many stones as the case would hold and then he snapped it shut.

He eased the man into the water.

They watched him sink. He stayed down.

He gathered up the soiled clothes and threw them into the bushes, the lenses and film along with them.

Then they hurried back to camp.

For the rest of it he needed a pick and shovel.

CHAPTER TWENTY-TWO

Saturday

"Where the hell is Graham?" said Caroline. "He's missing breakfast."

"I'm amazed he's up at all," said Kelsey. "I left him by the fire last night and he was fairly tanked. It was late."

"How'd you sleep?"

"Like a rock."

She nodded and poured the coffee. "I'm a little stiff myself."

"God, me too," said Ross. The eggs and roasted dinner sausage steamed on his plate. "I feel like somebody's been stomping on my back all night."

"Is his camera stuff gone?" asked Kelsey.

"Whose, Graham's? Yeah. Most of it is," said Ross.

Michelle stood up. The early sun caught her hair, turned it a deep red-gold. She put down her coffee cup and disappeared into the tent, reappeared with a jar of peanut butter. Caroline watched her open the jar and pour off the oil, then stir it with her finger as she walked back over again. She picked up a roll and split it and spread it thick. Then she licked her finger. Ross looked at her.

"I can't see how you eat that shit first thing in the morning," he said. "No way."

She shrugged. "I don't know how you can eat all that grease. There's good protein in peanut butter. In pasta too. Sometimes I have pasta for breakfast. It's high energy and it doesn't weigh you down. Good for the skin too."

"It's kid stuff."

"Pasta?"

"Peanut butter."

She sighed. "I'm just trying to educate you, Martin. You ever see a kid with hardening of the arteries?" She took a bite. "Finish up your grease."

Kelsey laughed and popped half a sausage into his mouth. Ross glared at him.

"So what's on for today?" said Caroline. Head it off at the pass, she thought.

Remembering last night and her comment about Ross she glanced at Michelle. They exchanged smiles.

"Whatever you want," said Kelsey. "No program. Swim, hike. Build a tree hut if you want. After we finish here I've got to cut some wood, though."

"I'll give you a hand," said Walker. "Haven't split wood since I was just out of college. I'd forgotten how good it feels. You remember what Thoreau said?"

Kelsey smiled. "Sure. Warms you twice."

"Wind sprints," said Michelle. "Wind sprints and yoga, then jump a little rope. Then swim. I was lazy yesterday."

"You're swimming?" said Ross. "In that?"

"It's daylight. We had no problem yesterday."

"You won't. Just stay out of the far end. The stagnant stuff," said Kelsey.

Ross shook his head. "I dunno. You're sure?"

"I'm sure."

He put down his empty plate. "It's going to get hot but I dunno. Fucking little vampires."

"Anybody see him go?" asked Kelsey. "Graham?"

"I didn't," said Ross.

"Not me," said Caroline.

Nobody else had either.

Caroline had woken only once during the night, and that was in the aftermath of a dream. In the dream she was home in bed and someone was scratching at the bedroom door, or maybe on the floor in front of the door, it wasn't clear which. So she'd gotten out of bed and walked over and opened it and there was her father, who was dying of cancer, who *had* died of cancer, but somehow it was also Kelsey. Her father was holding a baby.

"Come on in, dad," she said, "but leave the baby."

Her father just stood there staring. She woke.

She thought about that now and knew exactly what it meant.

Walker finished his coffee. "I have to tell you," he said. "I've got a confession to make."

"What's that?" said Kelsey.

"Birds," said Walker.

"Birds?"

"I like them—I mean I like to watch them. Jocelyn and I . . . it was something we did together. One of my guilty pleasures. I brought field glasses, actually.

That's why I passed on your hunt yesterday. That, of course, and the company of the ladies."

"Of course," said Kelsey.

"I thought maybe I'd take a walk down the path a bit. After we finish the wood detail. Care to join me?"

Kelsey grinned. "Birds, huh?"

"Yes."

"You've been reading William Wharton again."

"Not recently."

"And I can't bring the shotgun."

"No you can't."

"I figured. That's a rough one."

"I know."

"How about a couple of beers?"

"Those you can bring."

"You sure? I mean I wouldn't want the scent of Lowenbrau to put them off or anything."

"Beers will be fine."

"Okay, then. I'll come watch the birdies with you. But I want you to know something. This tendency in you shocks me deeply."

"I know it does."

He turned to Caroline. He shook his head. "My agent's a birdwatcher," he said.

"His client's an asshole," said Caroline.

They finished with the wood and Graham still wasn't back. Michelle was off somewhere racking her body with wind sprints. Caroline and Ross were down at the pond—Ross, at least it seemed this way to Kelsey, having overcome his aversion toward the leeches at the opportunity to try to insinuate himself back into Caroline's good graces. He wished him luck. One night three years ago Ross had gotten drunk and made a pass at Caroline, and he hadn't been in her good graces for five minutes since, though in deference to Kelsey she hadn't made a point of it.

"Ready?" said Walker.

"Ready."

They headed down the trail toward the stream where Caroline, Walker, and Michelle had waited while they hunted yesterday. About half a mile beyond lay the field. Walker kept watching the treetops and the skies. After a while, almost involuntarily, so did Kelsey.

"What are we looking for?" he whispered.

"You never know. Anything. Birds."

"There's one!"

He pointed to a tree nearby. A small brown bird on a lower limb. Walker looked.

"A sparrow. Honestly, Kelsey."

"Well, what do I know?"

"You know a sparrow."

"Yeah, I suppose I do."

"So? Do I make fun of your interest in jumping out of airplanes?"

"No. But you ought to."

"That's true."

They walked a while and occasionally Walker would point his binoculars into one tree or another but there wasn't much of interest yet.

"I wonder where Graham got to," said Kelsey.

"You know it's kind of odd. Morning's the best time for photographs yet here he is pissing one away."

"Unless he's photographing something else. Something other than you."

"That could be. He does a lot of nature stuff he tells me. But it's still a little odd to be moonlighting. We're his subject."

"You're his subject. Maybe he got enough yesterday."

"Maybe."

Alan put down the field glasses and turned to Kelsey.

"What are you telling me? You think we should worry?"

"I don't know. I guess not. He handles himself a whole lot better in the woods than I do."

"Yes, but even an experienced man . . ."

"I know. Anybody can fall and break a leg. Let's give it till we get back, say an hour or two. If he's not in camp by then we'll go out looking for him."

Alan nodded. "That's reasonable."

They walked slowly. The stream was only about a quarter mile away, and they were halfway between there and the campsite.

The trail was hard-packed dirt, barely wide enough for two men. Branches tugged at their shirtsleeves.

Ahead the trail narrowed.

Walker was intent on the sky so Kelsey fell back a few paces behind him. He really found it amusing. This urbane New Yorker out bird-watching. His agent. It suited something about Alan though, a feeling of briar pipes and tweed, a gentleness and gentility.

The trail narrowed further.

Ahead he saw a patch of dry leaves scattered across the path in front of them. He turned sideways to avoid a tendril of brambles. Alan, intent, oblivious, had already passed it by the tiniest of margins. He was a pace or two ahead now. Lower down another tendril scraped Kelsey's jeans.

They were coming to the patch of leaves.

The trail was narrowest here. Brambles poked out along either side. Overhead they formed a thin canopy. Alan had almost stepped into them and Kelsey was about to tell him to watch it when he saw him stop searching the trees in order to avoid the worst part. A big thick wicked-looking stalk hung right in front of him at face level. Thorns like cat's claws. Alan held it once he'd passed so it wouldn't spring back at Kelsey. Kelsey took it from him between thumb and forefinger.

Alan stepped forward as Kelsey edged carefully around the brambles.

He heard a shout and then a sudden breaking sound.

He let go of the brambles. They raked across his cheek. He felt his skin tear. He looked up.

Below him Alan screamed.

Where the leaves had been was an open hole.

It was maybe five feet deep, three feet square at the surface. Kelsey saw the remains of the thin wicker mat, the leaves and dirt that had concealed it.

Inside the pit Alan Walker writhed and moaned. The stakes impaled him like a grotesque wind-up doll malevolently stuck with pins. The doll was winding down. Five stakes, three square feet. They couldn't miss. They hadn't.

He knew suddenly who had done it and even why.

He lowered himself into the hole. He was shaking. Everything trembled.

"Oh god. Oh jesus, Alan."

Walker looked at him, eyes already glazing. Shock, he thought. He knew he had to move him fast. But how? One of the stakes passed upward at an angle through his side just above the hip. It was thick around as a silver dollar. Blood welled out of the wound and slid down his legs, stained his pants from within, spreading. The blood was dark. Dark meant arterial.

Another passed through his shoulder. The arm and fingers twitched ceaselessly as though charged with electricity. The head lolled back on his shoulder.

Kelsey's hands felt useless. Where to touch him? How to touch him? He looked at one of the stakes and saw that its tip was smeared with shit. *Infection, death*—primitive poison. He felt a moment of utter helpless panic. He clenched and unclenched his fists. He took a breath, bent down as far as the narrow space would allow and grabbed him around the lower hips and thighs. And lifted.

Walker's scream was high-pitched as a girl's. His body went rigid, then slack. His shoulder came free and blood splashed Kelsey's face and neck, pumped hot across his chest.

The second stake came up with him.

Kelsey saw the back of it scrape the wall of the pit. The sound nearly made him vomit, it burned the back of his throat. He choked it down. Walker was dead weight now but he hauled him up and out, trying to turn him as he did so, so that he'd fall onto his side and not onto the stake. But as he got the legs up he saw the tip of the stake touch ground and push through his back yet another inch or two, the dark blood oozing out fast across his midsection, dripping black into the dust of the trail.

He tried to jump out of the pit but he was too weak now. His legs felt rubbery. His trembling was uncontrollable. He kept scanning the trail, expecting the man, expecting to see him standing over them, rifle in hand.

He kicked down one of the stakes, kicked its point sideways into the wall and stepped on it. It held his weight. Grunting, he pulled himself out.

He rolled over.

Walker's eyelids fluttered.

Blood still pumped from his shoulder but the heartbeat was weaker and less steady now. Kelsey got to his knees and tore off his shirt. His eyes searched the ground, the scrub. He saw what he needed, a branch a few feet away.

He scrambled over to it on his hands and knees, knelt again and broke it in half across his thigh. It hadn't rotted much, there was still some strength left in the wood. He scrambled back to Alan. He got in behind him and lifted him as gently as he could into a sitting position, used his shoulder to support him while he tied the shirt over the wound, inserted the stick and twisted it like a valve.

The shirt had been pale blue when he began but it was red before the bleeding stopped.

"Alan."

He held the pressure on the tourniquet with one hand and with the other he lifted back his head and felt for a pulse in the neck.

There was none.

He had an impulse to try to slap him awake. Absurd.

I can't see your eyes, he thought. Don't do this. Please.

He let go of the tourniquet for a moment and angled around behind him so that he could see him. The eyes were open but the focus was wrong—one of them seemed to gaze off somewhere to the left while the other rode so high in its socket you could hardly see the pupil at all.

He cupped his hand in front of his mouth and nose, hoping for a hint of breath.

The mouth hung open. He waited.

An ant crawled up along his naked back. He let it crawl.

With a sob he shifted again behind him and wrapped his arms around Alan's bloody middle, held him loosely there. He pressed his head to Alan's head. He no longer worried or watched the trail. The stake in his side felt rough against his own bare flesh and for a moment it was as though they were both impaled there as he rocked him back and forth and let the tears come. It was still early morning and the birds were singing all around.

CHAPTER TWENTY-THREE

Lee watched him return to camp, staggering like a drunk and covered with blood but tougher now, stamped with hard knowledge.

They became much more efficient, he thought.

When they got that look they were dangerous.

Sprinkles never did, poor bastard, and that was why the night after the ville outside Cu Chi he had just sat there, sat in the dark in a firefight with rounds whizzing all around, no clip in his automatic, the clip just lying useless in his hand, sat there in his evil depression saying fuck it, fuck it, fuck it.

You had to get that certain look or you were in trouble.

This one had it now.

Pavlov sat restlessly beside him. He stroked the dog's head.

He watched the two women go to the man, saw their faces, heard the fear in their voices but also saw that they did not panic. The other man held back a little, ashen-faced.

A twink, he thought. Well he would learn too if he lived that long.

Which he doubted.

Time to draw them out now. Get them thinking.

"The Jeep," said Kelsey.

He washed off Walker's blood. The water in the basin was pink and his chest was still streaked in places but he couldn't stand doing it anymore. At least the sweet cloying stink was gone. He threw down the washcloth. "Get the shotguns and get in."

Michelle and Caroline went to the tents for the guns. Ross hesitated.

"What about Graham?"

"Graham's dead. If he never came back then he's dead. You can bet on it. Get in."

Ross's eyes were wide. "What the fuck is *happening*, Kelsey?"

"The farmer. The guy's a vet. Got to be. You remember the swing-trap? Well this one was a Nam thing too. Tiger pit—pungi pit. We need to get out of here, fast."

He walked to the Jeep and got in on the driver's side. He fished out the key and twisted it in the ignition.

It wouldn't turn over. Just a grating metallic whine. He felt something beginning to build in his chest and throat.

"The Mercedes," said Ross.

Ross ran to the car and jumped in.

Then that was whining too. To Kelsey it was a pathetic sound. Something slowly, inevitably running down.

They looked at one another. Ross's face was white.

Kelsey got out and opened the hood of the Jeep. He pulled off the distributor cap.

"God*damn* it!"

"What?

"Ignition rotor. He took the fucking ignition rotor."

He replaced the cap, slammed the hood down and walked to the Mercedes. "Open it up!"

He looked inside. His hands were shaking. "Yours too," he said. "The bastard's smart. Nothing we'd notice till we tried to get out of here."

Ross got out of the car. They looked at the old Dodge Aspen.

"I don't suppose . . . he forgot about that one," said Ross.

"Let's check it out."

He opened the hood and took off the cap.

"Gone," he said.

He closed it up. "I bet I can tell you what happened to Graham, too."

"What do you mean?"

"He had to have done all this last night. I left Graham by the fire last night. He was drunk."

Ross just stared at him. Then you could see it breaking.

"He was in here. Jesus. While we were sleeping."

"He had to have been."

Caroline came out of Kelsey's tent with Kelsey's and Walker's shotguns and a khaki travel bag. "All the shells are in here, right?" she said. Kelsey nodded.

"All but mine," said Ross. "Mich is getting yours."

"He fucked up the cars," said Kelsey. "We'll have to walk out."

"Then we'll walk," she said. No hesitation. Firm and strong. He loved the hell out of her that minute.

She handed him one of the Brownings. The other she held onto.

"Loaded?"

"Yes."

She gave him a handful of shells. He put them in his pocket. She pulled a fresh shirt out of the travel bag for him and he slipped it on.

Michelle came out of the tent and handed Ross his gun. "I couldn't find the shells," she said.

"I'll get them."

He ran to the tent.

"God," she said. "I keep thinking about Alan. About what you said."

"Don't," said Kelsey. He glanced at Caroline. For a moment she looked stricken. It would get worse later on, he thought, when it fully hit her that Alan was gone. Worse for him too. Already he had doubts about what he'd done back there.

But they had to keep going now.

"Don't, Mich," he said.

"I'm sorry."

They were silent. They watched the woods. Kelsey saw birds circling the pond somewhere behind them—probably on the farther shore—but apart from that there was nothing.

Ross came out loading his side-by-side 20-bore, a box of shells bulging his pocket. He snapped it shut.

"Okay. Ready."

"I'm not thinking," said Kelsey. "It's going to be a good day's walk out of here, maybe more. We're going to get hungry."

"Suppose we fill up one of the packs with food and water," said Caroline. "We can take turns carrying it."

"Good. We'll take the first aid kit too. And the flashlight. And the knives and hatchets. I don't know if we dare use the road. It's the obvious way out and he may have trapped it."

He looked at them but nobody volunteered an opinion.

"I don't think we'd better. Not this close to camp, anyway. We can cut back onto it a few miles down. So we'll want a compass. There's one in your pack, Caroline."

"I'll get it," said Michelle. "I know where it is."

She ran.

"And a bottle of scotch," said Ross. "I'm going to need a bottle of scotch."

"Then get it."

"You?"

"I saw that trap. I'm sober."

Ross thought about it. "Me too, then," he said.

"Let's get the supplies."

They went to the campfire. Ross and Caroline set their shotguns down side by side against a rock. Ross pulled the tarp off the tins of food and bottled water and gathered them up while Caroline sorted through the cooler. Kelsey kicked dirt over the smoldering remains of the fire.

He heard Michelle come up behind him. Walking slowly. Then her voice. She was very tense and quiet.

"Kelsey."

The sound of her voice warned him. He turned around.

The dog was snuffling the ground at the site's far perimeter. He was big and mostly black and Kelsey could see where a piece of the ear was gone.

The dog stopped and looked up at them. Kelsey had the shotgun cradled in his arm. He raised it now by slow degrees.

The dog took two steps forward. Its hair bristled. The eyes, the low angle of the head did nothing to reassure him.

He was aware of Ross behind him, moving toward their shotguns.

The dog growled and then stepped forward again.

"Don't," said Kelsey. "Stay where you are."

For once Ross seemed to be listening.

The dog stopped too.

"Shoot the fucking thing," Ross whispered. "Just shoot it."

His eyes locked into the dog's and he knew that it was not a stupid animal. The dark eyes glittered. The mouth was composed, close-jawed. There was no doggy panting. It was poised to move either toward or away from them and Kelsey knew that either way it would be fast and tricky, he could feel the tension in the lean hard body.

If the dog attacked directly he could probably kill it, all right. Shaking hands or not he still had a shotgun. But probably was not definitely and god help him if he had to reload. He would not want to bet they'd be there, all of them, when it was finished.

"I don't think so," he said.

"I'm moving," said Ross.

"No."

"It's the same dog, Kelsey. It's *his* dog. I'm not standing here."

"Yes you are."

"Fuck you, Kelsey."

The dog was snarling now, rigid, right paw leading, resting gently on the hard-packed earth—and Kelsey saw that it was ready, sensing their tension, its body hunkered low, teeth bared.

"Ross, I want you to take a real good look at that animal. You really think you're as good as he is? Then go ahead. Die. Die like an asshole."

Ross hesitated. Kelsey held his breath. Then out of the corner of his eye he saw Ross straighten.

The dog hadn't so much as blinked. The eyes were wide and terrifying. Lit with the intelligence of wolves.

Come on, he thought. You know what to do. Take the chance.

Surrender.

He took a long deep breath and held it and then gradually dipped the barrel of his gun toward the ground.

Something snapped in the bushes. Not like a twig. A human sound.

The dog straightened up and briskly trotted away.

Just like that, he thought. He felt the blood rush suddenly to his head.

For a moment there was movement in the scrub and then nothing.

He turned and saw tears on Caroline's face. She had never made a sound. Now she sniffed and brushed them away. Michelle touched her shoulder.

"Psychological warfare," she said. "Don't worry."

"It worked."

Next to her Ross's face was dark with fury. He was staring at the shotgun.

He looked at Kelsey. And Kelsey thought *yes it did work*.

Kelsey had the feeling he had three enemies now.

All of them declared at last.

—PART THREE—

CHAPTER TWENTY-FOUR

Be rational, thought Kelsey. It was not easy because the fear came in waves and he had all he could do to try to stand against them, he was capable of almost nothing.

He kept thinking about Alan. Alan's blood still filmed his chest. Alan's stink still clogged his nostrils.

He remembered the feeling of pulling him off the stakes, that sucking sensation, that sick resistance, and wondered if he'd done the right thing or if he'd killed him. Maybe he should have gone for help. There was doubt and he couldn't shake it.

He had excuses, justification. The arterial bleeding. The distance to camp. But when he let himself think he wasn't sure. Maybe Caroline or Mich would have known something he didn't, something that would have kept him alive. He thought about that now, watching them load the pack, and wanted to sit and cry again the way he had beside the pit, holding Alan's body.

No, he thought. Be rational. There was nothing you could do against that kind of wound. Be smart and think about now. That's what's important. The other you have to forget. Forget all of it.

Except one thing.

The pit had been dug in fresh earth. It was new, just a few hours old. It made him think that the man had only recently made up his mind as to how to handle them.

It was a reasonable supposition and you could continue from there. Time would be important now.

Okay, he thought. Figure it.

He'd gone to bed at three last night. Got up again around six, just after dawn.

Presumably the man was watching when he went to bed and just to be safe would have waited half an hour before entering camp to make sure everyone was asleep. That meant Graham could not have died before three thirty.

Given the need for silence, for careful movement, he must have spent at least another half an hour creeping around inside the camp. Yet another half hour, maybe, to dispose of Graham's body.

So that he couldn't have started digging the pit much before four thirty. The pit was five feet by three feet by three feet. He had to plant the stakes and cover it over. How long would that take? Two hours? Three? Even if it was only two that already made it about six thirty.

He and Walker had started out from camp about eight or so and hit the trap somewhere between there and nine—he didn't know for sure, but in any case he was back in camp by ten thirty or thereabouts, and the man and his dog were already in the bushes, watching. Between six thirty, the earliest the man might have finished the trap, and ten thirty was four hours.

That meant that if he'd gone out along the road, set another trap and come back, the furthest out he could have gone and still gotten back in time for the dog to make his appearance was two hours.

So if Kelsey cut west off the road and walked in a south-south-westerly direction for four hours, long enough to allow for rough terrain, then cut back southeast until they crossed the road again, they could reasonably expect to miss anything else he'd put out for them.

Unless, of course, he'd started earlier—before the killings. Or unless there was more than one man. But he didn't think there was more than one man or else they'd all have died in their sleep. Not just poor drunk Graham by the fire. He and Ross would have been next and then the women. As to starting out earlier he was only guessing but Kelsey didn't think he had. He still remembered the feel and smell of new damp earth.

The guy's moving fast, he thought. He'd made up his mind how to do whatever he was doing sometime during the day or early evening and now he was going after it.

That was better, he thought. Stay useful and you might get out of this.

You might.

Admit it. You want to run. All you want to do is to bolt and keep going until you run out of wind, and you want to run on a good clean road and damn the mines and damn the traps, you want anything but more woods. You want to get out of here.

The pack was filled. He hoisted it up.

"Let's go," he said.

They were an hour into the woods when Michelle had the feeling they were being *herded*.

She couldn't say why. Once they'd seen movement in the brush but when they'd gone in to look there was nothing there. It wasn't that anyway. Maybe it was just the nature of these trails, narrow winding deer paths that would disappear into the scrub and pick up again yards away. You wanted to hold to them because the scrub was thick and there were brambles everywhere. But she couldn't help thinking that if the trails were there and they had found them then the man would know them too, would figure where they were going and was maybe even leading them there.

It was simply a feeling. Of being watched, of not being alone out here.

She was always very aware of someone else's eyes on her. In the studio she did not have to look to know where the camera was. She knew where it was exactly. She even knew what it was framing. Upper body, portrait, full body. On a runway she knew where the important buyers were, where the press were sitting and where their eyes were going. You had to in order to play them. Long ago she gave up on public gyms because in a workout you didn't need that feeling. It was distracting and irritating. And nearly always there. Because she was beautiful, because her body was what it was, she got stares and sidelong glances. She got them a lot. And sometimes she could find where the eyes were across the most crowded dance floor in Manhattan if she wanted to.

Someone was watching them now. She was sure of it.

The sweat along her backbone was running cold because of it.

But she couldn't find him. She searched the trees and brush to either side and silently cursed him.

She felt vulnerable without a gun, and having Ross behind her didn't help any. Ross was just as likely to shoot her by mistake as he was to shoot an attacker. Ross was nervous and jumpy and sullen.

She wasn't used to this feeling.

Vulnerability sucked and she was scared.

Maybe I can deal, thought Ross. I must have something the prick wants. Not the marijuana. Hell, he can't really care about that. Even if he does I can explain that it was Kelsey who wanted it, and if he knows Kelsey—who didn't?—he'd believe me. I bet he would. So maybe that was what he had to deal with. Kelsey. The Big Star. Maybe he was like that Hinckley character. Or that guy who got Lennon. A star-fucker, a star-killer.

He considered for a moment what would happen if the guy got Kelsey. He was pissed at Kelsey, sure, but he didn't know how he'd feel if the guy actually got him. Killed him. Right in front of his eyes. He didn't know how he'd feel about that.

Or maybe he liked the women.

You could hardly blame him there.

Whatever. There had to be something. Everybody

had his price and whatever it was he'd find it. He was getting out of this. Alive. The rest of them could just go take it up the ass if it came to that. Actually he was a little excited. The shotgun felt good to him.

He was living.

They were moving through a clearing sparsely studded with pine, looking for a path through the heavy brush. The fresh tang of pine sap was so normal as to be almost reassuring.

Don't kid yourself, thought Caroline.

Why am I so calm now?

She'd been trying to grasp it and it still eluded her. She, who considered herself so firmly grounded in reality, so bottom-line practical minded, was having impressively basic trouble believing, for instance, that Alan was dead, that he wasn't here beside them, strolling and talking as they walked through the woods. She couldn't picture him dead, much less dead in the way Kelsey had described him, bleeding, speared by stakes smeared with dogshit. Worse, she could not really fathom the obviously essential reality that there was a man out there apparently hunting them for little or no good reason, that he meant to kill them at some point during the day today, at his leisure no doubt, and that somehow he'd already managed that with the photographer. And Alan.

She kept coming back to Alan.

How could these people be dead? She'd just seen them. They were strong and healthy, laughing. Just the night before. She knew what she knew but she couldn't *feel* it. How in the world could you kill over a few stupid leaves of marijuana? She knew it happened, but now that it *had* happened and to people near her, she couldn't even absorb it enough to fear it thoroughly.

Oh, she was scared all right. Her throat was dry and her legs were shaky. But not scared enough. Not as scared as she should be. She had a sense of unreality about this that just wouldn't go away. It didn't make sense. They were walking in a stand of pine with needles underfoot, birds twittering somewhere, and squirrels in the trees. It was noon and they were not insane, the world was not insane, no one had dropped The Bomb or burned off the ozone layer or repealed the standing laws on abortion.

So?

So you are holding a shotgun, she thought.

Will you use it?

She considered that a moment.

Yes. Given the opportunity and the need, she believed she could do that, she could point it at a man and shoot him. If she hit him some part of him would then explode into blood and bone. She knew that. And still she thought she could.

So the world had gone crazy after all. Some of it had,

"Found it,'" said Kelsey and they proceeded up the trail.

Lee watched them from a hillside half a klick away and everything was as he'd guessed, right down to their formation. Just as it all had been.

The timing wasn't certain but that had never

mattered. Whether it began by day or night was irrelevant. What was relevant was that they were doing what he expected them to do.

The psychology was simple. People in essentially unfamiliar surroundings who felt in no particular danger always took the most familiar route to get anywhere. That was why he'd dug the pit where he had. He'd seen them use that trail, as well as the one on the way to his crop. So there was a pit there now too. He'd known that sooner or later they'd use one trail or the other and he'd get one of them and that would make four, and four was an easier number.

But then you proceeded to think further. Once they *did* feel threatened it was just the opposite. They'd avoid any route they'd already taken. They were bound to become more cautious. Especially if they knew they'd been watched, their movements plotted.

The part that was tricky was back at the campsite. He'd had to lure them out of there. Threaten them but not too badly. That was where the dog came in. Get them moving.

There was a simple psychological reason to do it that way too.

If you were attacked on familiar ground you tended to scatter. You forgot you might be alone after that, you were used to feeling secure in that area and you didn't think. You just ran. You ran fast and hard.

So that back at their camp, if he'd told the dog to kill or wasted one himself that would have been the reaction of the survivors. They'd have scattered.

Tracking them all might have been a problem. He was only one man. One, maybe even two of them might possibly have eluded him.

Whereas here in the woods, in unfamiliar territory, even under attack they would tend to cling together for security. The *area* was threatening. He could take out one, and three would hold together. Take out one more and two would.

He put down the field glasses. He could see them with the naked eye.

It was easier this way and more efficient.

They had no idea where they were headed now. Just some compass point west of the road.

He did.

CHAPTER TWENTY-FIVE

McCann stood by the shed and scanned the hillside, his sensitive eyes squinted into slits against the sun. The pot was curing nicely. Its thick earthy smell wafted over him and reminded him of summer, as it always did, of Washington drying out at last—and also of Nam, the jungle after a rainfall where the raindrops got so big they hurt you, that steamy scent of fresh-watered green.

He crushed out the half-smoked cigarette and reached into the shed for the scotch. One o'clock and I'm hittin' it, he thought.

He unscrewed the cap and took a pull on the bottle. The whiskey burned through him and for a moment he couldn't smell the dope anymore. Then it dissipated. He capped the bottle and squinted down the hill again. He pulled out a Lucky and lit it with a new disposable lighter. Then he uncapped the bottle and drank again.

How come, he wondered, scotch tastes better in the sun?

How come I'm fucking standing here?

He'd returned to the Hollywood apartment Wednesday evening and Grace wasn't there and neither was Matty, and he'd thought about Lee. An hour later they were back with bundles of groceries and a new Masters of the Universe guy for Matty, this one with an ejectable tongue for god's sake, and the kid had thrown his sweet soft five-year-old arms around daddy, around McCann, and again McCann had thought about Lee.

He thought about him off and on at the Exxon station Thursday where he worked as a mechanic, at the Limelight that night where he drank and dealt a little weed, and then back home in bed with Gracie. And maybe it was Grace, making love to her and thinking about him afterwards and feeling pretty lucky all told, lying there between her too-big beautiful thighs, thighs as big and substantial as McCann's were, that did it to him.

Shit, the guy was Nam. In Cu Chi they were buddies, grunts in sister outfits through some of the worst sweeps of the war. McCann went all the way back to basic and AIT with the sucker and what was he doing to help? *Nada.*

In Nam you'd see a guy fucking up and you'd have one of two choices. Ignore it, forget it, and then stay the hell away from him because fuckup was likely to get you dead—or else help the sonovabitch, try to set him straight. A grunt would trust another grunt and you could do something. In Nam he'd have taken the shot with Lee, he'd have tried. *Listen, what's on your mind, asshole?*

So what was different? This wasn't the Nam. This was The World god knows. But that wasn't much excuse for dumping what you'd known was right over there, for turning into another greedy selfish prick who'd piss on his buddies for the price of a Japanese gardener.

So Friday at the garage again he thought about it. He worked on remembering the terrain and figuring the four or five places Lee was most likely to be. He pretty much had it down now. He was supposed to have taken Matty to the San Diego Zoo but he'd put it off a week, done this instead today, and Matty didn't seem to mind. When McCann left, He-Man was bashing away at Skeletor on top of Snake Mountain.

It was going to be a touchy thing. He knew that. Damned touchy, and it troubled him. Because chances were good that Lee had forgotten, as much as he had forgotten, that men could be decent to one another, take care of each other without really prying and without condescension, leaving them with their pride. For some reason he had never figured out the confidences that came so easy over there were a whole lot harder here.

So it was going to be a very touchy thing.

He remembered wondering, looking at him Wednesday, if Lee had done anything to his wife and son. If he had, McCann sure as hell didn't want to know about it. But he supposed he would just have to know. That was maybe part of it. The wrong you did was part of you too. And you had to be accountable. The point was, it was worth a shot.

He was seriously worried and he wasn't worth shit if he didn't try.

He wiped his beard, capped the bottle and stuffed it into his ruck. He had a change of clothes in there, a couple sandwiches wrapped in foil, and a knife and compass. Should be enough, he thought.

He stared down into the forest.

Too damn bright up here, he thought. Good for the dope but not for me. Fucking malaria.

He supposed it was as good an excuse as any to get his ass down off the mountain.

CHAPTER TWENTY-SIX

Okay, thought Lee. Snare's ready. Nice and simple. Now to the other thing.

He walked to the woodpile.

Too bad you couldn't be sure they'd come that way, he thought. There was only one other though. He could watch that.

And wishing got you nowhere. Hell, it was too damn bad he had no firearm with long-range capacity. They'd all be dead by now.

And then what? he thought. Doesn't somebody come looking?

There was no point worrying about that.

The dog moved back away from him as he raised the axe.

They crossed a brook, moved slowly through a patch of brambles, and found the trail again on the other side. The going was easier here, the path wider than before, and they were able to walk two abreast. Michelle moved up beside Caroline. They were coming down into a depression, a gully, and judging by the

214

smoothness of the stones it looked as though a stream had run here once, perhaps the sister stream to the one they'd just crossed. It was mostly bare rock with tufts of stringy grass between.

I hate this, thought Michelle. It's too exposed.

"Kelsey?"

He turned to her and nodded.

"I know. I don't like it either."

"Hurry, okay?"

The air was still and the sun weighed down on her as they crossed, so that she was grateful for the shade on the other side as well as the cover.

The path continued wide through the scrub. Ten minutes later they came to another stream. She wondered if either or both of them fed into the pond at their campsite. She wasn't much good at directions.

"Got to get rid of this pack," said Kelsey. He unbuckled the padded waistbelt and slipped it off his shoulders. Under the pack his shirt was soaked with sweat.

"Ross?"

"Yeah. Sure. Why not."

Ross stepped forward and Kelsey helped him on with it, then checked the lashing on the flashlight and the khaki travel bag where they were keeping the shotgun shells.

He tugged at them. The lashing held. He stretched.

"God, that feels good."

He checked the compass and then his watch. "Another hour or so, then we cut over."

"We cross?" said Ross.

"Yeah."

He handed Ross the compass. Ross put it in his pocket and took the lead.

Kelsey walked past them to take up the rear. "How are you two doing?"

"Tired," said Caroline. "Otherwise fine."

"Mich?"

"Starving."

Kelsey looked at her.

"I know. It's ridiculous."

"Wait till we get to the turning."

"I can wait."

The stream lay thin and shallow on its high banks and was easy to cross. On the other side Ross extended a hand to her and she took it. The gesture was unexpected but under the circumstances it was welcome.

"Thanks," she said. Ross said nothing.

A dragonfly darted past her. She waited for Caroline and helped her up.

Like the first brook this one was surrounded with thicket too but Ross pushed his way through it as though it were an affront to him. Michelle passed easily in his wake. The thicket gave way to trees and brush, moving down an incline into what seemed, ahead of her, to be a clearing.

Ross stopped.

"I think we got a break," he said.

She peered over his shoulder. "What is it?"

"Not sure. Kelsey?"

Kelsey came up beside him. "Looks like an old logging road, a fire trail or something."

Ross checked his compass. "Runs due south. That's parallel to the road. We can take it and make some time."

"That is a break," said Kelsey.

The trail was just tall brown grass now, the grass at least shoulder high. But there was nothing else out there except a starved-looking bush now and then.

"A break? No it isn't," said Michelle.

"Huh?"

"That's a break? The guy's following us, isn't he? Aren't we assuming that? Look how open that is. The streambed back there was nothing compared to that."

"It is," said Caroline. "It's awfully open."

Kelsey studied it a moment, then shook his head.

"It's better than you'd think," he said. "That grass is good concealment. I've hunted in the stuff and you can barely see three feet ahead of you half the time."

"That's great," said Michelle. "Suppose he's three feet ahead of us?"

"Hiding in the grass? He won't be. He knows we've got shotguns. Shotguns are made for that kind of killing. Honestly, we're better off in there than running up and down hills where he could just as well be behind the next rock or the next tree. If he's crazy enough to hide in the grass then he's like a game bird in there, he can see less than we can. The trick would be just to stay together pretty tight so he can't pick anybody off, jump up and knife a straggler or something. He could try something from the brush or the trees along the sides but if anything happens you drop, and he doesn't know where you are.

"The thing is, this isn't easy country. I'd like to get

back to the road by nightfall so it would be good to use this. I'll leave it to you, though. If it's going to make you crazy walking through there we'll stick with the rough stuff."

"I'd risk it," Ross said.

Caroline looked at the trail again. She nodded. "I suppose," she said.

So it was up to Michelle then.

It wasn't a position she liked. She didn't trust her judgement now and it was like the feeling of vulnerability, she wasn't used to it at all. She felt clenched, tight, the muscles of her back constricting.

"Look," she said. "I've been feeling somebody watching me all the way through this. Every step. It's been beating the hell out of my nerves so I don't know what to say exactly. I could be paranoid. But he's out there somewhere and we know he's not stupid. I just wonder if there isn't some way he can use this, take advantage of it."

"He's had the advantage all along," said Caroline.

It's true, she thought.

"I don't know."

Do I have to say yes to this? she thought. Why don't you all just trust me? She felt like an animal scenting fire in the air. Something strictly of the body said stick to the woods. But the body had no words, no reasons, no good arguments.

"All right. I guess we go, then."

Ross turned and moved through the trees, stepped out into the grass, and she followed.

The earth felt spongy underfoot. Shallow mud sucked at her boots. The grass was taller than it looked, more than shoulder high—it sprang back in their faces. Its dusty pollen tickled her nose.

She had not been aware of mosquitoes before but now she slapped at one on her neck. She waved away a gnat and then another. Kelsey was right, it was good concealment, but she didn't like it, not at all. The heat was oppressive, damp, and she smelled decay, the old dead grass and mud beneath her feet.

She stayed close to Ross and felt Caroline and Kelsey walking side by side close behind her, heard the light liquid sound of their footfalls. She heard insects buzzing, whining past her, and the rustling of grass, but no birds at all.

This was faster, yes. The ground was flat and there weren't any brambles to worry about, no thickets to plow through—but the sweat and pollen made her itch. In fifteen minutes she felt grimy. The sun carved deep into her scalp. She could hear Kelsey's labored breathing.

The sense of being watched never left her. The sense of being *herded*.

She concentrated on her breathing, working the muscles of her abdomen. She snatched at bits of tunes in her head but couldn't hold on to them.

It was half an hour before they stopped to rest.

Ross sat down, his back to her, offering her the pack. She unzipped one of the big compartments and took out a plastic quart bottle of water, opened it, drank, then handed the bottle to Caroline. Then she cupped her hands. Caroline poured water into them and she worked it into her hair. Her headache receded slightly.

She found an apple and an orange in another compartment and ate the orange greedily. The apple she held for later. She passed crackers and quarter-pound chunks of cheese to Caroline, Ross, and Kelsey.

If I were free, she thought, if I were alone, I could run my way out of this. I could be on the road in no time.

But she wasn't free. She looked at Kelsey. He still was breathing heavily.

Cigarettes, she thought. He's got to quit.

Funny what you think of.

Five minutes later they were up again slogging through muck and grass.

She itched incessantly and the sun bore feverishly down.

Half an hour later they saw the smoke.

CHAPTER TWENTY-SEVEN

"What is it?" said Caroline.

"Campfire," said Ross. "It's got to be."

The smoke was thin and gray, a broken column ahead of them to the west in the bright sunlight.

"His?"

"I don't know," said Kelsey. "Could be."

Caroline watched him weigh the angles. He would do that. It was familiar, characteristic. She remembered how he would look when fly-fishing, studying the possibilities, looking for the perfect spot, his brow wrinkled, frowning, lips turned down and pressed together tight in concentration—all this just to cast. He was the same way mornings at the typewriter.

"It's hard to tell distances," he said. "But I make it about a half mile away. Not far off the trail. Somewhere near that last brook we passed, possibly."

"It could be his," said Michelle.

Mich was scared. She'd said that—and her eyes, the tension in her body, her tone of voice had not stopped saying it since.

And sure, Caroline was nervous too. But mostly she

was excited now. Wood smoke might mean a stranger, a camper, a car. A way out.

It could also be him.

Blocking? Am I blocking?

"It could just as easily be a ranger or something, couldn't it?" she said. "Somebody who could help? We've got to look, don't we?"

Get me out of here, she thought. She wanted to be clean, she wanted to be safe, read a book, watch television, drink the night away—anything.

There was shit smeared on the stakes, Kelsey said.

You are blocking, she thought. You are. Well, go right ahead. It could be anybody. Believe that.

"Bernie?"

"I don't know. If it's him, why would he have a fire going? He'd be out here watching us, wouldn't he?"

"He likes traps, Kelsey," said Michelle.

"Okay. *When* then? When would he have time to build one? I mean if he's been watching us like you think he has. And who's to say we'd come this way? It really could be a ranger. There are plenty of them out here. There'd be a radio, transportation. We'd be gone in no time."

"It's not a ranger, Kelsey."

Yes, thought Caroline. Yes of course it is. You don't know. It could just as easily be. *You can't know.*

She felt suddenly angry.

Just get me out of here.

"We could be careful, come in slowly," said Kelsey. He looked at Ross. Somehow that surprised her. Thus far it had been as though Ross's opinion didn't matter much. As though he were barely there. So

222

now Kelsey surprised her a little because it was not the kind of considered response that would follow his weighing the angles, was not what he did with the fly rod or at the typewriter.

"What do you think?" he said. "Can we afford *not* to?"

"I think it shits," said Ross. "But I think we ought to see."

She could have hugged the little bastard.

CHAPTER TWENTY-EIGHT

There was no good way to approach it silently because the brush was too thick once you got past the stream so they did the next best thing, they approached it with shotguns up and safeties off, and Kelsey thought that that might do unless the guy had a machine gun with him in there—and despite the alarm running through his bloodstream he still thought the most likely thing was that it was just a camper, maybe one with transportation who could get them safely to the road. He told himself that.

Ross had the pack so Kelsey took the lead. He reasoned that you'd need somebody who could move fast if he had to, with no extra weight on him.

So he was the one who broke through first and saw that the camp was pitched in a sort of blind at the end of a narrow trail, surrounded by woods and thicket.

Nobody home, he thought.

The tent was old, had seen plenty of wear. The flap was open and he could see inside. There was nobody there. Some clothes were hanging on a makeshift clothesline. Men's clothes, he thought. He saw a ghetto blaster, a book and a tobacco tin beside the tent. The book was open.

The fire was burning low toward the back of the site. It was not a good sign because what kind of fool would leave a campfire burning unattended out here? Only someone new to the woods. And the tent belied that, the tent was used and old.

He watched and waited. He had a bad feeling about this now, a gnawing in his belly that was like hunger. The fire bothered him. But give it a minute, he thought. Maybe the guy is off taking a piss somewhere.

And there he was.

Tall thin guy in a bright red shirt and blue jeans, coming toward the fire through the trees, carrying a tin plate and cup, walking up from the stream.

Carrying the lunch dishes.

A little late for that because the shadows were lengthening now. But no weapon on him and nothing crazed or hostile in the way he moved that Kelsey could see. No dog, either. Guy in his late thirties, strolling into camp easily and naturally, an everyday thing.

It had been almost too much to wish for but maybe they had some luck after all.

Give it one more minute, he thought. It couldn't hurt. He didn't think the man had seen him yet and it was better to be careful. So watch what he does. Watch carefully.

He was aware of Ross moving up beside him, a tension in him at first at seeing the man there but then relaxing just as he was relaxing while the man put the dishes inside the tent, got the tin of tobacco and tossed another log on the fire, then sat down and started to roll.

"I think it's okay," Kelsey whispered.

"Yeah?"

"Yeah. You notice? No dog."

"Uh-huh."

The man lit his cigarette, picked up a stick and poked at the fire.

"How you want to do this?" Ross whispered.

"I guess we just announce ourselves."

He looked over Ross's shoulder to Caroline and Michelle. "It's all right," he said softly. "Come on up."

"It is?" said Michelle. "How do you know?"

"No dogs. No guns. It's okay I think. Come on up."

"I don't think so. I'll wait."

He felt suddenly impatient with her. He knew it wasn't fair but he'd been under plenty of pressure too and he couldn't help the excitement now, the pressure was releasing finally and enough with her attempts to frighten him.

"Suit yourself," he said.

Caroline pushed past her. She was smiling and the smile was a little wild.

This is happening just in time, he thought. Things are cracking.

"Easy," he said. "Let's not scare him to death."

They stepped out into the clearing.

The man sat hunkered near the fire. Smoking, oblivious. His profile was sharp and solid looking.

"Excuse me," said Kelsey.

He took a step forward.

The man started, looked at them, grinned, and then stood slowly, almost awkwardly, leaning over as he did so—so that his right arm dipped out of sight for an instant behind the fire.

And Kelsey stood there like a deer in the headlights of an oncoming car, frozen, trapped by the eyes of the man as he picked something up off the ground—trapped with the blood rushing fast to his head, crushing his instinct to run, trapped by a look in the man's eyes that was suddenly awesome and deadly and, strangely, he thought, ultimately more caged and frozen than he was. Awestruck as though those eyes had looked into some horribly distorting mirror and seen himself alone there, and Kelsey wanted to yell mistake! you're mistaken! I know this! as the man straightened up and finally—a strange black agony of separation for Kelsey—swept all three of them with his gaze and made his choice, cold now, professional, and pointed what might have been a gun at them except that it snapped and hissed and thudded into Ross like a striking snake.

Ross wheeled toward Kelsey with the impact and dropped the shotgun and Kelsey saw the dart like a hi-tech, multicolored playback of the stake piercing Alan Walker's side, and that was when he fired, both barrels, forefinger fluttering on the trigger. Never aiming and hardly even looking at the man who jumped and rolled behind the campfire. His shots exploded into the flames. Sparks, ash, and chips of burning wood erupted all around the man but nothing seemed to touch him.

He was up again fitting the second bolt into the crossbow as Kelsey fumbled in his pocket for shells.

Caroline's shotgun sounded and he looked at her, saw Ross facing her, clinging to her with his hands on her shoulders like a huge praying mantis as the gun waved high above them, firing again uselessly, the recoil spinning it violently out of her hand as she almost tripped and fell. He saw blood fly off her hand.

Ross's face had gone nearly purple. He clung for an instant and then Kelsey could almost feel the pain in his side as he wrenched her out in front of him.

"No!" Kelsey screamed, whether to Ross or to the man he didn't know because he saw what Ross was doing, he was using her as a shield against the bow.

He looked at the man. The man was aiming.

He fumbled a shell into the shotgun.

Behind him something crashed in the brush.

He whirled as he heard Michelle scream, sudden and sharp, and saw her on the ground and saw the dog on top of her. Her hands groped deep into the dark thick fur of its neck. Its hind legs straddled her. Its forelegs raked her shoulders. He heard the big jaws snapping.

He whirled again, torn. The man was aiming.

The man fired.

Ross hurtled back as though sucked suddenly down through a wind tunnel. His backpack slapped heavily against the tree behind him and his neck and head snapped with it. Caroline fell, sprayed red. Ross shuddered against the tree, arms and legs jerking. Only for an instant. Then Kelsey's eyes found the bright red stain sliding down over his mouth, over his chin and neck and he thought inanely, Ross has got a nosebleed. Then he focused better and saw that the nose was gone, shattered, and in its place the man's second blue-feathered dart passed back through the base of his skull and pinned him to the tree.

The man was on his knees behind the swirling dust of the blasted campfire, working with the crossbow.

He turned back to Michelle and saw the blood across her cheek where the dog had scratched or bitten her, he saw the plaid cotton shirt torn wide off her shoulder and the deep red claw marks that started there and angled down across her arm, her underarm and breast, saw the grim hard set of her jaw as she struggled, muscles straining, holding the great shaggy head up and away from her. He saw tears and sweat streaking her face, and something went coldly joyous inside him because this much he could do, this he could accomplish, and he took one step toward her and pointed the shotgun to the dog's torn ear, noting how raggedly it had healed over.

He angled the gun barrel carefully between her hands so as not to harm her and pulled the trigger.

The head blew apart and it was suddenly as though she were holding a bloody heap of fur and rags that splashed itself down over her.

He whirled again and the man was on his feet. And he saw that the bolt was for him this time.

On the ground beside him Caroline took aim with Ross's gun and winced as she pulled the trigger.

The man flew back behind the fire. The bolt hissed high overhead.

"Come on," he said. His throat felt thick with sudden bile. He lifted her up.

They turned toward Michelle as she climbed out from under the ruined carcass.

He took her arm and jerked her to her feet and they began to run.

CHAPTER TWENTY-NINE

His first shot had not been a kill shot and that was why the dog lay dead now. It was his fault, he'd been overanxious, overconfident, or else something about the heavyset man had disturbed him and thrown him off. Something like that and now the dog lay destroyed in front of him his brains speckling the brush.

The dog, he thought. Say his name. Why can't you say his name?

"Pavlov."

There.

Good. *Now say Sprinkles.*

Shit no. No. That was insane, there was no damn need to put himself through crazy stuff like that just because the head . . .

He stared at where the head had been.

Meat.

You could smell it.

Go ahead. Say *Sprinkles.* Say it.

No way.

But it all came back to him anyway. *(Fuck it.)*

Sprinkles the night after the ville outside Cu Chi. Sitting there in the dark.

Lee stood looking blankly at the dog, dimly aware that his shoulder was hurting, peppered with gravel where the woman's shot had slapped against the stones of the campfire, which had shattered the buckshot and flung it up at him like shrapnel. Looking at the dog whose name was Pavlov. *(His son was called Lee Jr. His wife was Alma.)*

Looking, thinking *Raphael David Stern* whose name for all of them then was Sprinkles.

All day long he'd brooded. Lee knew what he was brooding about but no one could make it better. The dinks were in the area for sure, at least the ville had proven that, so the sweeps went on all day but Sprinkles was just diddy-bopping, he didn't seem to care, staring at his shoes half the time with the M16 pointed at the dirt.

That same night their squad had gone out on night ambush, humping through brush that wasn't dissimilar to this, under a moonless sky—and four klicks out of their firebase they crossed a VC unit, a big one, out doing the same damn thing.

What happened then was everybody's nightmare, a wild blind firefight where Charlie knew the terrain and you didn't, where the radioman was almost the first to go and nobody even knew where he'd fallen so that there was no way to call in Arty support or gunships or even a medevac chopper to haul out the wounded. In the first few minutes of fire there were four of them wounded and three of the ten of them dead. Those who were left saw quickly that they were surrounded, a rough circle of fire coming in from everywhere, pinning them into the pitiful cover of grass and shrubs and the few shallow holes and trenches they'd been able to round out with their routing tools. Fire was a constant roar, everybody shooting everywhere because you didn't know where anybody was except for what the tracer bullets told you and because everybody was panicking.

After a while they got low on grenades and clips so they held back and firing became more erratic, everybody socked in tight to where they were, and he and Sprinkles had it pretty good all told. He'd scraped out a low narrow trench in back of some thick brush and they were better there than most. Henderson lay a few feet away behind a rock no bigger than a basketball. Clemons had nothing but grass to protect him—they found that out the following day but they couldn't see him now. They didn't hear him either until Lee recognized his voice a few minutes later, which was maybe a few hours since the firing had begun and the VC started moving in on them, tightening the circle, taking them out one by one.

"No no no," he heard Clemons say, and then he said, "please, you got to . . . please . . . " and then they heard a burst of bullets. Even Doc was silent listening to the sound of Clemons's voice begging them not to kill him, and Doc had been constantly screaming, gut-shot, somewhere to the left of them.

That was when Sprinkles sat up. Right after Clemons died and Doc started screaming again.

"Fuck it," he said. "Fuck it." Clearly visible behind the scrub.

Lee reached for him, grabbed hold of the pocket of his fatigues and tried to pull him back but Sprinkles

233

just shook his head, slapping at his knuckles with an empty clip and murmuring way down into his chest until Lee heard the AK47 fire and Sprinkles fell back into the trench.

It was worse than any of the others because, he guessed, they'd been together for so long and Lee had done what he knew you were not supposed to do, he'd assumed that they'd get out of this year together the same way they got in—live and whole. He even knew Sprinkles's middle name by then, it was David, which was what they called him back home because nobody liked Raphael for a name and Sprinkles had wondered out loud how he'd gotten it in the first place, but nobody in his family wanted to remember.

So it was bad, very bad, and Lee pulled him over and saw where the bullet had angled up through his neck. He applied pressure to the carotid artery like he knew he was supposed to do and opened Sprinkles's jaws to apply mouth-to-mouth. And there was just enough light to see his brains in there like a pile of bloody dark half-digested stew in the back of his throat.

He threw up on Sprinkles's shirt.

And then he heard Doc die. A short burst of fire and no more screaming.

He fired in that direction until the clip was empty.

A few minutes later he heard Scag get wasted and then Henderson behind the rock. His clips were finished by then and so were those he'd taken from Sprinkles but he still had the one grenade when he heard the rounds chipping away at Henderson's rock and then heard him scream. After that there was just quiet.

As far as he knew he was alone out there.

He heard the thin nasal babble of the VC unit as they moved around through the brush finishing off the wounded.

He climbed under Sprinkles's body and lay face-down, clutching the grenade with both hands under his neck, ready to pull the pin. He'd made up his mind that he was not going to beg. He twisted his legs painfully so as to look as dead as possible and lay there, listening to the stream glide over the rocks nearby.

The VC were being careful. It was an hour later before they got to him.

By that time the cold blood sliding slowly down his back could have been his own.

They poked at Sprinkles and then they poked at him.

Satisfied, they left him alone.

He lay under Sprinkles's body until the medevac chopper arrived at dawn.

He'd been afraid to move his head enough to look around, afraid they might still be out there some-where. So he lay there smelling Sprinkles's blood and brains and piss and shit for three-and-a-half hours until daylight and when the medic pulled him out from under he damn near blew the grenade because he was so completely out of it by then he didn't even hear the chopper. He *was* dead.

And he stayed dead for days. He stayed dead until they sent him home amid a pile of GI coffins.

Then there was the bar fight, and then he walked.

He looked down at the dog and realized he'd done it again, he'd gotten attached without half knowing it.

It was such an easy, natural, stupid thing to do. The dog was a good dog and they'd taken care of one another. The dog had even taught him things.

He remembered when he and Alma had gone to the ASPCA and picked him out of the litter, so small Lee could hold him in the palm of his hand. He'd been born on the street behind a grocery store and you could see the street still terrified him, because they'd sat on Alma's mother's couch looking out the window that first day and the dog's eyes got wide and he'd tremble every time a car drove by. And Lee could relate to that. So he sat there and stroked him, stroked him for hours, getting better and better at it, adjusting his touch to the body weight of the dog and the small fragile bones, trying to make the dog feel good, calming him until he fell asleep across the back of the couch.

And from then on the dog didn't tremble anymore when he looked out the window, you could see he felt safe and protected finally, and Lee realized that the dog had taught him how to touch something well and gently again, had given him back his hands so as not to frighten but to comfort. He was amazed it was even possible.

He looked at the ruined carcass now and thought of the nights he'd wakened crying and hysterical and the dog would be lying half across his lap. Staring up at him. Giving it back.

He took off his shirt and draped it over the dog. He felt old, drained, exhausted. This is the last one dead, he thought.

He went to the tent and picked out an unopened

bottle of scotch and broke open the cap as he walked back to where the dog was and then raised the bottle. He toasted the dog and drank. Fuck of a dog, he thought. You deserved a better man.

He remembered the dog's dark eyes in those early days staring fascinated and newly confident down onto the street that had frightened him and knew that he would never do anything that useful again, and when the sobbing finally reached him he was already on his knees, the liquor pouring out into the dirt, the bottle falling from his open hand, alone.

CHAPTER THIRTY

McCann walked the path down into the clearing and congratulated himself. His third guess was right. Because here was Lee's camp and here was Lee, digging.

The digging made him cold.

He wished his eyes were better. He could see something lying behind Lee in back of the hole. Lee was standing in the hole and it was about three feet deep he judged, but whatever it was it was lying in the long shadows and he couldn't see.

What or who it was.

He approached slowly and wished he'd brought his shotgun. What if the guy was past it? Then what?

Nah, he thought. It's Lee. Stop worrying.

Just to the left of the trail as it widened out into the blind there was a stand of tall, second-growth pine, and he registered that one of these trees must have been hurt bad by wind or storm because it leaned out past the others over the trail itself, and as he came to that he could see Lee better and was relieved.

It was the dog he was burying, Pavlov. That was truly a fucking shame. But it was a whole lot better than Alma or his son.

He called him. "Hey Lee! Moravian!"

Lee's head darted up and he hauled back the shovel like a weapon. But it was the look of him that stopped McCann, not the shovel. That look was cold.

"Shit, Moravian—it's me, McCann!"

And he was about to follow that with something like sorry about your dog when he saw Lee's glance shift to the side, over to the stand of birch trees opposite the leaning pine beside him, and he followed the glance and saw in the shadows what he guessed he'd been afraid of seeing all along. Some poor bastard tacked to the tree like a butterfly. Soaked with blood to the navel.

He'd seen dead men before and they held no power over him. Dead was just dead and there were worse things. It didn't make him scared or frightened or anything. He didn't really think Lee would want to try to hurt him no matter how crazed he'd gotten. He doubted that. He'd gamble on it. He just felt so fucking bored and sad and tired all of a sudden. Sad for Lee and this damn fool guy here, whoever he was. Sad for his own pitiful raggedy-ass self, dealing the dope and hitting the bars and trying to be a daddy. He felt sad for all the guys over there who died and all the ones who didn't die, whose wounds were still so gorgeously technicolor wide open because nobody'd ever bothered enough to do the fucking work to close them up again. It was all a fucking stupid waste.

Tired and sad, sad and tired. It was like music, the everyday music of his life. He heard it every day.

Now there was another thing. One more.

He took a step back toward the pine and shook his

head. He looked at Lee in the bright sunlight and thought, the guy's a ghost already.

And he was about to take another step into the shade, to sit down and rest for chrissake, when he saw Lee's eyes flash wide and his mouth form a strangely soundless *no,* but he took the step anyway, he was in the middle of it, and felt himself kick something, a piece of wood, and suddenly his legs went out from under him and he was upside down, swinging wide away from the leaning pine tree that was not leaning now anymore but had snapped up straight and he thought, *rabbit snare, I can't believe I fell for that shit,* as he saw the trunk of the tree looming toward him on the backswing, coming at him like a freight train. He put out his hands and had time to hear his bones snap for an instant before his skull shattered against the tree trunk and he bounced and swayed

CHAPTER THIRTY-ONE

The dog kept coming through the brush at her even though she knew the dog was dead. Her hands and arms were iron red with its blood. Her sweat made it moist and sticky. What was coming through the brush behind her was only Caroline and Kelsey. Still she heard and remembered.

She had to struggle with the urge to distance them. Fear wanted to propel her forward—it wanted her at top speed. Fear and practicality, too, seeking the path of least resistance toward her ultimate survival. She held them both in, and asserted her will instead. And her will was to stay with them, not to negotiate away the unit.

Who says we're a unit? she thought.

I do.

So the dog like a Fury snapped at her heels.

Her will kept it there.

She pushed them hard. It was late afternoon. They would not be able to run much longer.

In her mind the road lay ahead of her like a four-lane highway swarming with traffic, not the narrow dirt track it really was, that led, eventually, to a winding rural tarmac in poor repair. The road was man-made, human, built by people of sane and practical reckoning for others to use, in order to give them freedom, even hope. A road could lead you anywhere. To Chicago or New York. It did not have the deep inevitability of the forest where trees fell and rotted in exactly that position their growth had determined in the first place. With a road you could choose your place to die.

She pushed them knowing that the man would push himself as well now, that the dog's death had changed things and the game of cat and mouse was over. The dog's attack had shown her that. There had been no signal that she could see. Yet the attack was timed directly to the man's need like a sixth sense running between them. You did not get that from an animal without caring. Its breath, even as its teeth had torn her cheek, had been fresh. Its coat had been rich and clean.

The man would want them badly now.

So she kept them at a run whenever there was trail enough to allow it. She knew they both were hurting. She could hear Kelsey's breathing and saw when she turned that he was favoring his left leg. Caroline was running better than that but the shotgun's kick had probably broken her index finger. They hadn't stopped to splint it and she held it to her chest, Her face was drawn in pain. Michelle had Ross's shotgun now. She thought of Caroline firing it at the man and wondered how she'd been able to do that even with Kelsey's life on the line. You just did things, she thought. You had pain and you ran with it, took it, accepted it, warmed to it, and tried to go through it to the other side.

She ran them hard. It seemed forever.

The glow of sunset at her back burnished the scrub ahead of her and then fell away, turning things flat and gray by slow degrees. After that she could only hope that their direction was right because the compass was gone, back in Ross's pocket, and it was impossible to go straight ahead exactly through the brush. She wondered how good Kelsey's sense of direction was. She wondered if he'd stop her if she went too far one way or another.

How far west had they come? How far to get back? How much time before the dark made every step treacherous and they'd have to stop completely?

She wondered where the man was.

Night was coming and he would follow but she had no sense of him now. She thought of him moving through their campsite. She thought of Graham. The man was good in the dark. It was almost enough to make her wish to face him now while there was still daylight and food in their bellies and not too much exhaustion.

No, she thought. Push them. Push yourself. Buy us time and distance and maybe we'll fool him and live and the scar on my cheek will heal and it won't be enough to stop me working and building the house in Arizona for us and the claw marks will heal too and Caroline's hand and this will just be a horrible memory three days from now.

I wonder how the baby is? she thought.

I wonder if it's scared.

She embraced that pain too like all the rest as the darkness folded down.

CHAPTER THIRTY-TWO

He stumbled, fell, caught himself with the butt end of the shotgun and hauled himself up, something soft and wet in the heel of his left boot tearing. *Blisters.* He supposed there was blood now.

He was tired in every joint and muscle and the road would not appear. Impossible to have overshot it. But for all he knew they were running parallel to it, not east. In the dark he couldn't tell. It was cloudy and he couldn't find the Dipper or Polaris. He knew there was a way to tell from Cassiopeia too but he'd never learned it.

Some woodsman, he thought. Graham would have known.

"Stop. You've got to stop," he said. It came out small and he knew they hadn't heard him. But there wasn't any point. Not anymore.

His lungs felt raw and overheated, his heartbeat like an aching tooth. His heel felt scraped to the tendon.

That's it, he thought. I quit. I can't see a thing. I can't walk. Any minute now I'll be running into trees. He stopped and knelt where he was, leaning on the shotgun.

"Mich!"

Two dark forms stopping, turning toward him.

In the forest even they were frightening.

"That's enough. Find a place . . . for the night."

"You all right?" It was Caroline.

"Yes. Just . . . let me . . . get my breath. Just a minute."

He looked past them into the darkness and for a moment he seemed to see the man behind them, swaying, holding something that glinted like metal. He gagged on his own ragged breath. But there was no moon to see by nor hardly any stars, nothing glinting, only bright lights whirling inside his eyes, and the man was just a broken trunk of birch tree that Michelle, moving slowly back into the darkness, now leaned against, looking down at him panting like a dog into the rich loamy earth.

CHAPTER THIRTY-THREE

Caroline would have given anything to be deep inside a cave now. A fire at the entrance. No, they couldn't have a fire. He'd see that. But a cave.

She knew this was the best they were likely to find in the way of shelter but god! it wasn't much, just a space inside a thicket of brush and brambles big enough to lie down in and with just enough head room so that you could sit hunched over. The brambles were heavy and went back a ways on every side except the one they came through, and that meant the man couldn't see them there except directly on, where they would see him first—and they still had their shotguns.

She knew they had no choice. You couldn't go on blundering through the dark. A broken ankle would be a disaster now. Even Kelsey's blisters were a problem. He thought they were bleeding. But he wouldn't remove the boot to see, afraid that in the morning he might not be able to get it on again.

Afraid. Kelsey was afraid.

She could sense it in him. In his posture, his voice. His confidence had deserted him at some point since they'd started running. She wondered if Michelle sensed it too. She thought it over and decided it was probably the choices he'd made since they broke camp this morning that were bothering him. That would be like him. Avoiding the main road. Handing the gear over to Ross (she could still feel Ross's hands on her, cold, desperate). Allowing them to be lured toward the smoke.

But in her own mind his choices had been reasonable. Michelle had argued against the campfire and as it turned out she was right but there was no way to have known that then for certain. She thought he had nothing to regret.

Of course what she thought didn't matter.

It made her feel lonely. So that it was almost good to be hurting, to take her mind off things.

And she did hurt. Her index finger was broken somewhere and possibly the one beside it. The webbing was torn between them but by now that had stopped bleeding. Michelle had pulled off the sleeve of her shirt where the dog's claws had ripped it and then taken two thin strips off that and found a pair of sticks to use as splints. Now as she tied off the second strip the pain raced through Caroline's body like an orgasm.

At least the way she remembered orgasm.

"Bad?"

She tried to smile. "Not too bad."

"Liar. You have shells in your pockets?"

She nodded.

"Give them to me."

She handed them over. Four of them.

"That's all?"

"Yes."

Michelle put them in her pocket. "Kelsey?"

"Five. With two in the gun." He shrugged. "Seven."

"Jesus."

Caroline sat up, reached for Michelle's chin, and turned her face so that she could see where the dog had gotten her. She was thankful that even in the woods at dark of the moon the eyes eventually registered some light. She could see, for instance, the pale flesh of Michelle's arm, the shadowless curve of her breast and her rib cage where the shirt seam was torn.

"How's the cheek?"

"Throbs like hell. I'll live."

Listen to that, Kelsey, she thought. *I'll live.*

Her meal ticket possibly shot to hell, scarred, even if she does get out of this. There's a cut on her cheek here the size of a bracelet. Dirty and untreated.

So what's an honest mistake or two compared to that? Listen and learn. Life is bigger than your failures.

You should talk, she thought.

Hell, it was probably a mistake—an honest mistake—to have never had Kelsey's baby. Your mistake, not his or hers.

And you'd make somebody pay for that?

Life is bigger than your failures. Shit.

Michelle settled back, leaning on her elbows. Caroline saw her breast roll away from the shirt, saw the darker nipple and the claw marks there.

She stared at the wounded breast. She frowned.

She turned to Kelsey.

"You sure about that boot?" she asked. "You sure you don't want to take it off awhile?"

"Yes."

"Is it all right to talk, do you think?"

"Probably not," he said. "No."

His voice was listless, almost a mumble.

She was silent then but it was hard to just sit and stay that way. The forest groaned and whispered. No arms reached out to comfort her and no familiar sounds were there to lull her off to sleep. She wondered if she was exhausted enough to sleep. She wondered if Michelle felt as she did, that Kelsey had isolated himself from them now just when they needed him and each other most, that it was unfair and brutal and childish of him. Male, impossibly male.

He had rarely acted that way. Despite the public image and even his private pursuits he was not that kind of man, normally. Not the sort to fear his more feminine side, the side that shared even the bad things, that cared and accepted care, that nurtured. But he was ignoring these things now, he was being a man, just another man who'd failed to do what men told themselves they were supposed to do—protect, be strong, be *right*—and this was the worst possible time for him to start.

She had the sudden urge to cry. To shake him.

Wake up, goddamn you, she thought. How dare you ask us both to love you with you in a cage and us outside, taking care of things?

How dare you?

She heard movement in the bushes in front of them. She started.

And Kelsey was taking care of this much, his shotgun was up and firing before she'd even finished flinching. A red-yellow blast that blinded her for a moment and roared in her ears.

Except that what ran off into the brush was not even close to man-sized.

Beside her Michelle was trembling. So was she.

And so was Kelsey. One vibration that ran through them all together.

Fear.

Is that where we stand? she thought. Is that, finally, all we really share here?

Her ears were still ringing when Kelsey lowered the shotgun to his lap and said, "You can talk now I guess."

His voice was sad and cold and distant.

Michelle flared at him.

"Bullshit, Kelsey."

For herself she had nothing to say. Michelle had said it for her.

For a while they just sat there.

Then he said, "I think we'd better hold each other. Okay?"

And that was better.

CHAPTER THIRTY-FOUR

Thanks, thought Lee.

He turned toward the sound of the shotgun, walking faster because he knew they were not nearby. He missed the dog. The dog would have had them by now or had the scent at least. But the gooks had killed the dog so he guessed he'd just have gooks on a fucking mess plate. Fucking ears and eyes and little dink cocks. Reparations.

Thank you very much. You just made my life a little easier.

He took his time. He had all night.

For them it was going to be a long one.

Chapter Thirty-five

Saturday Night / Sunday Morning

Caroline thought of the city. L.A. and Boston and New York. She closed her eyes and she could see the brownstones and tree-lined streets, the Pan Am building all lit up at night, cars whizzing by on the freeway. She went shopping in Soho. She went to galleries. She browsed through America Hurrah, sipped a Manhattan at Chasen's. Ice tinkling in the glass. The cool night air was vibrant with the voices of frogs and crickets, contrapuntal, washing over them in thin percussive waves. She was dirty. She could smell herself, damp and sour. Her hand was killing her. But you could only be scared for so long like you could only mourn the dead for so long before the brain went into overload. She thought of the city.

She wanted to cry.

She wanted to confess to Michelle about the baby.

Michelle, who did not fall in love with cruelty. Like she did.

She might even need Michelle.

Who could say.

She wanted Kelsey to confess too. Before it was too late. To his fear, to his shame. *Give me an hour talking with him and I can make them go away.* She wanted him to tell her why he wanted her and Michelle too—that again—as if that were important now. Hell, she *knew* why. Because people were not some Aristotelian half-circle creature wandering through life looking for the other half to make them whole. The model was wrong. People weren't *solid*.

There were hundreds of empty spaces. Thousands. They were shot full of holes. Someone came along and put a finger here, a finger there, and you bled less, and it helped. But no one could stop up all the holes.

She knew why. She knew how what happened to you young could make you permanently lonely. She only wanted to hear it from him. Clearly. Once. Now.

Tell me what I do for you. Tell me how much. Make me know how important it is and I won't worry about Mich anymore. I swear it.

She wanted to talk but it had been hours since they'd dared. It would be morning before they dared again.

She listened to them breathing, one on either side of her. She listened to the crickets and frogs.

I hate the woods, she thought. The woods doesn't give a damn. You die in the city, drop dead on the street, and a crowd gathers. The crowd takes care of you. They cart you away.

They do here, too, she thought. There were ants, maggots, blowflies. The crickets reminded her.

An animal would sleep now. Lightly, attentively. But sleep. Go out in the morning and find the road, refreshed.

Anybody sleeping here?

She looked at Kelsey. Then at Mich. The sound of her head turning in the brush was almost too loud to bear.

She closed her eyes again and the Mass Pike drove fast and sweet and even.

CHAPTER THIRTY-SIX

In the hour before dawn the temperature dropped and Kelsey lay shivering beside his wife, the forest gone so black he could see barely half of what he'd been seeing all night long now. His eyes were tired and they wouldn't adjust anymore. The air felt crisper, more rarified in his lungs as though the forest floor had raised them up unnoticed to a different altitude. He wanted to light a cigarette but knew he couldn't risk it.

The cold was making him shiver but it was nerves too. They'd been up all night with no food or water and he felt like a college sophomore who'd crammed all night on coffee and dexedrine. His tongue felt swollen. His lips were parched and flaking.

He knew that if he had a mirror to look at and a light to see by the eyes would look red and strange, drugged, staring. They stung when he blinked. He'd look at himself in the mirror and think, is that me? He tried closing them awhile and then opening them again but they still wouldn't pierce the darkness. He remembered the man's eyes back at camp and thought, that is the loneliest man I've ever seen.

There was darkness and there was darkness.

He closed them and opened them, closed them and opened. They still felt dry and unrelieved.

—PART FOUR—

THIRTY-SEVEN

They saw him just before dawn.

The sky was beginning to brighten. His shape was dark against it and Michelle saw him at the edge of the trail coming slowly through the brush, fifty or sixty yards away. She edged forward and raised the shotgun.

She felt Kelsey's hand touch her shoulder.

"Never," he whispered. "It's too far. The Browning, maybe. Maybe."

The man was crossing the trail now.

"You want to let him pass?" she whispered. She could hardly contain her sudden fury. She looked at him and saw the conflict last only a moment.

"No. We may not get another chance. I'll go for it. Get ready to run if I fuck it up." He looked around. The brush was thinner up the trail to the left. "That way."

She watched him click off the safety, then kneel. His hands were steady. He raised the gun and sighted carefully.

The man was across the trail and moving into the brush.

Now, she thought.

Kelsey squeezed the trigger. The man twisted and seemed to dive into the bushes.

The shot echoed loud in the morning stillness. Above them birds screeched and flew away. She scanned the bushes. She could see no movement.

"Did you hit him? It looked like you hit him."

He stood and lowered the gun.

"I don't know."

They stared down the path into the brush. Wisps of fog trailed over them. She was aware of Caroline standing next to her. Nothing moved.

He fitted a shell into the shotgun. She was counting. One last night and one now.

Eleven left between them.

"I guess we'll have to go find out," Kelsey said. He turned to Caroline. "You want to stay here? It might be safer."

She shook her head. "I don't want us to separate."

"Okay. Stay behind a little, though. You too, Mich. Don't bunch up. Easy now."

He led them down the path.

She knew why he'd warned them. The urge was to stay close for the feeling of security it provided but she resisted it. They'd be easy targets that way if the man was still alive. She stayed back six feet or so and watched the bushes. Her clothes felt damp and cold.

They'd gone maybe thirty yards when Kelsey stopped. He turned to her and pointed left.

It was an angry gesture—frustrated. He shook his head. Like he was disgusted with something. It confused her for a moment but then he started walking again and she followed and when she got to where he'd been standing she looked. And knew exactly what he meant.

Jesus Christ the road. The fucking road.

She could see it down through the brush and trees, less than fifteen yards from where they had spent the night.

There all the time.

Freedom.

All they had to do was walk now. Walk and stay alive.

She pointed so Caroline would see it too and kept going, giving her attention back to the bushes.

They were close. Kelsey moved slowly. One step at a time and then stop. One step and stop. The sky was brighter, grays working through to greens. It was impossible to tell exactly where he'd fallen but it was somewhere nearby. Very near now.

A breeze tugged at the tear in her shirt and she shivered.

The man erupted from the bushes.

She jumped.

Jumping saved her life.

He was diving, firing, a yard back into the scrub. She heard the whistle-hiss of the dart sail past her chest. She fired and cut away the scrub in front of her.

Kelsey's shotgun roared in tandem. She could see the man roll to his feet again almost even with Kelsey now, running zigzag through the scrub and she fired again, her finger jerking on the trigger. No, she thought. Squeeze on him, take your time.

She broke open the gun and dug into her pocket for two more shells and jammed them into the chamber.

Kelsey was already after him. He bolted into the scrub.

The man ran clean and low as though there were nothing in front of him but a clear dirt track. He was running on an angle toward the road ahead. Kelsey stopped and fired. The man kept going, fast, agile as a rabbit. She saw Kelsey crouch to reload and began running along the path, roughly parallel to the man, running hard, angry now and wanting this over with, willing to shoot him or drive him forever if she had to, thinking of the road—and when she got to where she was just ahead of him she stopped and fired, squeezing this time.

The man never looked directly at her but must have seen her stop or sensed it because he rolled again and all she hit was the brush behind him.

Furious, she fired again, and when the man got up she was sure of it—he was grinning.

The bastard was grinning. Laughing at her.

He raised the crossbow and she threw herself down onto hip and shoulder.

He's drawing our fire, she thought. That's all he's doing.

She broke open the shotgun and chambered her last two shells. Her hands trembled. Save them, she thought. Be careful.

She got to her knees and saw the man near the road and Kelsey blundering after him.

Stop it! she thought. You're too easy! All he had to do was turn and fire. She snapped her gun together and followed them.

The man veered away unexpectedly from the road back into the scrub, into a stand of trees.

For a moment she lost sight of him and then there he was again standing behind some evergreen, watching, not even breathing hard. She couldn't shoot. Kelsey was still right ahead of her, crashing through the brush. She saw the man raise his weapon.

"Kelsey!"

She saw him start to fall and she knew his timing was wrong, knew he was too slow. She saw the man fire and Kelsey fall to one side as the dart crashed into the brush behind him and then saw blood pour out over his forehead, rolling down in a sheet over his eye and cheek, and she forgot her resolution to be careful with the last two shells and fired at the man in a screaming rage, fired twice in rapid succession, sending perfect hate careening out along with the shells. Tree bark and blood exploded from where he stood somewhere down at thigh level. She saw the man slide down behind the tree and then she ran to Kelsey.

CHAPTER THIRTY-EIGHT

No problem, thought Lee. Chunk of thigh meat. Nowhere near the femoral. Slow you down a bit but not too much.

He sat down behind the tree and unsheathed his K-bar. He cut off his shirtsleeve and tied it tightly over the wound.

He'd loosen it later when the bleeding stopped.

Two half hits made one whole. Not too wonderful a performance but not bad either dodging a batch of shotguns.

You're getting old, though, he thought.

But he'd chosen right and the asshole with the ruck had all the shells and supplies. Now all they had was what was in their pockets. It couldn't be much. He'd know when they were empty. He'd make them empty.

He could have wished for better luck than to run into them like this, them in the dark and him cut out against the morning sky. But generally speaking the location was good, he could turn it on them now because the road was so near and they needed the road, they'd be hungry for it, they'd stay close. It'd be hell on morale.

He wondered about the heavyset guy. How bad he was.

Now or later, he thought.

He strung the bow and checked the spare quiver lashed to his belt.

The fog was lifting.

He remembered the smell of gooks—old bad sweat and medicine. He was smelling it now. The breeze coming off them bore it straight across the years like beehive rounds that delivered their thousands of small projectiles and pierced him everywhere.

CHAPTER THIRTY-NINE

It was Caroline running toward him, running low. He saw two of her with his good left eye and tried to wipe the blood out of the other. The blood just kept on coming. He tried to get up on his knees but everything tilted on him and he fell right back on his ass again. He wiped at the blood.

"It's all right. Stay there. Don't move."

She got down beside him and unbuttoned her shirt and pulled it off. The shirt had once been white. Very dirty now. The bra still was white unless he opened the other eye and then it was red.

She rolled the shirt and pressed it to his forehead.

"Caroline?"

"Wait."

She put one hand over the shirt—the hand with the broken finger—and put the other hand in back of his head and pressed.

Heal.

He felt all right, nothing hurt him. A little light-headed, maybe, a little drunkish. So where was all this blood coming from? Why was he fucking bleeding here to death?

He turned and somehow Michelle had come up beside him too. She was doing something. Picking up his shotgun.

He didn't remember dropping it.

Now digging in his pockets. First that one, then the other. Putting something in her pockets now.

Pocket. Singular. One pocket.

What was that down there?

Snake?

Shit! Oh god! Shit!

No snake. A shotgun. Her shotgun. Okay. Got it. I got hers and she's got mine. We're swapping.

Why?

Who the fuck knows.

Back to Caroline. Caro-line.

My god, he thought, she looks horrible! Is that from me? From seeing me? Something's *that* bad?

"Caroline? Hey listen. Am I . . . ?"

"Shhhh."

He felt the shirt lift away and saw her wince. Michelle was looking too. The shirt was bright red now, with or without the eye.

"How do you feel?"

"I . . . dizzy. Weird."

It came back to him then—where he was. Why he was there.

"He got me, didn't he?"

"He sure did," said Michelle. "You've got a hard head, Bernie."

He grinned. Spinning again. Whirling. "You love that about me, right?"

"I do now."

She was looking back to the trees, the shotgun in her hands.

He felt the warm strange wetness sliding over him again. The eye pooling. Caroline pressed the shirt down. Didn't that hurt her? The finger? He felt a dull throbbing pulse somewhere inside his head. Their voices seemed very loud.

"I see him," said Michelle. "I see the bastard. Over there."

"What's he doing?"

"Nothing. Standing by the tree. Wait. He's moving. Damn it!" She turned to Caroline. "Can he walk, do you think?"

"I don't know." She lifted the shirt. "God! There's so much blood." She pressed it back again.

"Head wound. They'll bleed forever. Look, we've got a problem. You see him? He's back of those trees there, heading toward the road. Once he gets to the road we're cut off. We'll have to stay here or else . . ."

"Go back?"

"Go back, yeah."

"Don't want to go back," said Kelsey.

"Oh god."

"What else can we do? We can't stay here. There's no cover. Weeds and brush. You want to wait for nightfall again? No food, no water? With him out there?"

"Couldn't you just . . . go after him?"

"Not with four cartridges I can't. I'm not that good, Caroline. God! I'm terrible with this thing! As far as I can see all we've got going for us is that he doesn't know we're down to four cartridges so he's got to be careful. But we're not doing the hunting anymore. We had our chance and we blew it. He's the hunter now."

"Again," said Kelsey.

"Again," she said. She looked at him. "What do you think? Can you walk?"

"If you get me to my feet. I think I can."

IthinkIcanIthinkIcanIthinkIcan. The Little Train That Would. Could.

"All right. Hold on a minute." Caroline turned the shirt inside out and rolled it, pressed a fresh side to his forehead and tied it tight with the shirtsleeves.

The throbbing began in earnest.

He put his arm over Caroline's shoulders. They felt tiny, slim—warm and comforting but strangely unfamiliar. He tried to stand but his legs were all funny, his feet splayed. He tried again. He looked at Michelle. Mich faced the trees with the shotgun. No help there.

Okay, *up* goddammit.

The legs felt distant and jointed in places he knew they weren't supposed to be but they held him.

He looked at Caroline, the brown skin of her shoulders, freckled where the tan was heaviest, the face lined and set and worried looking. The skin felt very smooth. He remembered the amber body oil she used, back on the ledge in the shower. He thought she looked ten years younger.

He gave himself the command to walk.

He put one foot after the other.

CHAPTER FORTY

"Oh jesus," said Michelle. "You see what he's doing?"

She was aware of Caroline and Kelsey turning around behind her. They'd been working their way slowly through the scrub, parallel to the road heading back to the campsite, and the man had been following at a distance through the brush on the other side.

Not now, though.

"He's daring you," said Caroline.

"He's crazy. I've got a shotgun."

"He doesn't care. He's daring you. He wants you to try."

The man was standing in the middle of the road forty to fifty yards back.

Just standing. Completely exposed.

It was tempting.

"Maybe he thinks you're empty."

"Keep going," she said. "Screw him. He wants to play, let him come closer."

It was a strain though. Backing through the brush, keeping him in sight. It was easy for him. He could take one step on the road for every two of theirs. He had clear level ground to walk on and he wasn't hauling wounded. Kelsey was doing all right so far but every so often his legs seemed to go and Caroline wasn't strong. She should have been the one doing the hauling. Certainly she should not have been the one with the gun. That was fucking absurd.

It made her angry that it was so easy for the man. He was pacing them. Stalking. A war of nerves and he was winning.

Just come a little closer, she thought. I'll blow your head off.

She could see him clearly now. Not bad-looking in a way but blank, expressionless except for the eyes. Late thirties, early forties. Hard in the body. Long arms and big wide hands. Tall. He was favoring his left leg and she could see where she'd shot him.

Not once had she caught him blinking. How could you stare like that? How could you maintain it? Was he crazy? He looked crazy. She knew that the eyes would tell her first if he was going to move so she knew she had to watch them. But she didn't like to. Nobody had ever looked at her like that before. It was as though she were not a human being but some sort of math problem, some sort of geometry. The eyes were scary. The eyes would start her trembling.

She was trembling now.

She knew that Caroline had seen them too and she was trying to make Kelsey move faster now. But it was awkward in the brush. She could hear them, feel them stumble. Walking backwards it was hard to keep from stumbling herself. She wanted the road.

She worried about Kelsey's head wound. It was deep. When she'd looked she could see to the bone.

Down to the goddamn bone. Kelsey needed the road too and the man was the one who had it.

She began to slow down. Smaller steps. Let them get out ahead of her slightly.

You want a confrontation? You think I'm empty? Come closer.

The man did. He was careful, he was watching—but he did.

More, she thought.

"Mich?" Caroline was looking over her shoulder.

"I'm all right," she said softly. "Keep going."

"I think I can see the campsite."

"Good. Keep going."

"I can see it."

"Good."

It's a seduction, she thought. Think of it that way. Bring him in close enough to get a decent shot.

She stopped.

The man stopped too.

She backed away but more slowly.

The man moved closer.

Thirty-five, maybe forty yards now.

She could see the bow was fitted with a dart and there were three more in some sort of quiver attachment below it. Half a dozen more hung from his utility belt. The man moved like a natural hunter. Like he'd done this a thousand times. He was a vet, Kelsey said. She was probably crazy herself for thinking of going up against him this way. But she had agility. She could move too when she had to. The thing would be to keep on leading him until they were near the campsite and there was some sort of shelter—the Jeep, whatever—for Caroline and Kelsey. Then do what he'd done. Fire and roll and be up and firing again.

The man stopped.

"That's enough," he said.

CHAPTER FORTY-ONE

Caroline turned and felt Kelsey sag beside her. She knew it had been very hard for him and perhaps this was the end of it now. Perhaps this at least was relief.

Her back and shoulders were slick with sweat. They ached.

His voice had been surprisingly gentle.

For a moment nobody moved.

Michelle held the shotgun steady at waist level. To shoot she would have to bring it to her shoulder because otherwise there was too much risk. The man held his crossbow away from him, pointed at the ground.

Kelsey moaned.

She risked a glance at him. She was shaking from exertion and fear and looking at Kelsey made it worse. It was better or had seemed to be better while they were moving. Now he looked bad. Pale. Losing too much blood. He needed a doctor, a hospital, or at least direct pressure or stitching. You couldn't wrap a shirt around a wound like that.

His head rolled slowly away from her. His eyes were closed. His mouth hung open.

She felt suddenly close to panic. Overwhelmed. Like she was melting in the sun.

The man. The weapons. Kelsey. All of it too much.

Michelle and the man stood motionless. Some tiny, almost imperceptible change between them in the moment since she'd glanced away. Some heightened awareness. She could sense it—something very near now.

She wished for it. An end to it. Alive or dead.

She wished the man would speak again. It made him seem more human. Maybe they could think, could talk, could reason.

Kelsey's head drifted toward her, brushed against her naked shoulder. She felt sticky wet cotton.

His legs went out from under him.

There was too much dead weight and both she and Kelsey were slick with sweat and blood. She couldn't hold him. She felt a sharp jolt of agony from the broken finger as she tried and failed to close her grip on his arm.

He fell.

And then it was as though Kelsey were the timer to an explosion. As though all the clocks in the world went off at once.

Grasping for him she went to her knees amid brush and stones and heard the shotgun roar, looked up to see the man diving toward Michelle into the direction of the blast, knowing instantly what he'd done as the shot spread out far above him, that it was like moving inside a fighter's punch and that he was close enough now for his own shot so that she was not surprised when it came, not surprised but sick inside at the power of the thing as the dart slammed up through Michelle's hand gripping the gun stock, splintered the dark wood, and tore through her opposite shoulder as it ricocheted away, still arcing upward, spinning.

Mich twisted and fell and the man was up, coming at her.

She saw this and her good hand clawed the earth, searching.

The man was running, fitting another dart into the bow.

Caroline stood up and knew that for this one moment only she had the advantage. The man was running at an angle to her, concentrating on Michelle in the tall grass and on the bow. The rock felt good and substantial in her hand. She crossed behind him. She swung it at his head with all her power.

The man turned, sensing her, tried to duck, and the rock caught him just above the temple. The rock jolted away somewhere into the brush. The man fell, rolling. Let go of the bow, she thought. But he didn't. She looked frantically for the shotgun, for another rock—anything!

Michelle was on her knees, clutching at the wrist of her ruined hand.

"The shotgun!' "

Her face was white with pain. She shook her head. I *don't know*.

Caroline looked at the man. The man was writhing, groaning. Did she dare?

It was like reaching toward a dead thing or a rattlesnake.

Revulsion. Terror. But she had to have it, she had to try. Her hand closed over the crossbow and she pulled.

For a moment she thought it was hers.

The man's grip tightened. It was fierce, powerful, frightening. She could feel his strength like a thunderclap in a dreadful night sky. She screamed and let go and ran to Michelle.

And out of the corner of her eye saw him rising.

CHAPTER FORTY-TWO

"Come on."

"Kelsey . . . where's . . ."

"Come *on!*"

Her torn shoulder sent pain like stab wounds throughout her body but she was able to raise the arm and Caroline wrenched at it, pulling her up.

She almost fainted.

The man was on his knees. Blood glistening on his scalp and matting his hair. They ran.

The road was just ahead. There was no more chance of hiding. She stumbled on a rotten log but kept her footing and then they were on the old dirt track and she could see the campsite ahead, the Jeep and the Aspen and the Mercedes that seemed to belong to a thousand years ago, like familiar strangers.

Each step pounded at her hand and shoulder.

She felt weak, legs shaky. Weaker even than that time two years ago—that really bad flu. *Remember that flu?* She wasn't running well. Not well at all. Couldn't summon what she needed. What she really wanted to do was to just lie down and hurt and cry but Caroline was up ahead of her leading her and Kelsey . . . where was Kelsey?

She wanted to lie down but the man was just behind them and she'd lost the shotgun.

She'd lost it.

She remembered the dart again, like a freight train coming. Metal against bone.

She was furious with herself and weak and shaking. How had she lost it? Why? How could she possibly have let it go?

She remembered the moment of impact, played it over and over. The *sound*. The crack of bone and wood together, so near her face, the brief sudden slicing, carving, sawing against her shoulder.

It was fear that did it. The man was killing her. Pain told her that. And pain made fear. Fear made her drop the shotgun. She had damn near tossed it away. It was all so fast, so easy.

And Kelsey?

She turned. The man was on the road. He had just stepped out of the brush.

I hate you you prick you bastard.

The man was running. Much too well.

Well fuck it so could she.

"Caroline!"

She ran wide around her. She took the lead. Behind her Caroline ran faster.

The camp was just ahead, just a few yards away—but what was *there*? What did they have there that could help them? Her head felt clearer now but she could think of nothing. They'd taken all the guns.

And the knives, the hatchets—they were all in the pack or strapped to the pack and the pack was gone.

"Wait."

The axes. They'd left the axes.

Where?

And how could they use them? *Caroline's fingers. Her own shattered hand.*

Never mind, she thought. Just find it. Remember.

They ran past the Jeep.

She thought of Kelsey and Walker splitting logs first thing in the morning, right after breakfast. There.

"Caroline!"

She veered toward the tent that was Walker's and Kelsey's and saw the stump and the cut wood and one of the axes still propped beside it. She lifted it. Her shoulder protested its weight. She lifted it anyway.

She had an idea.

Caroline was beside her but Caroline was much too small. She'd have to do it herself.

The problem was the crossbow. At any kind of range they were dead. She'd have to get in close. She had to surprise him somehow.

"The pond. Hurry."

They ducked behind Kelsey's tent and then across to the one she'd shared with Caroline. She could see him coming past the Jeep.

Walking in now, looking for them. Taking no chances.

They slid down the incline behind the tent and walked through the bushes to the lip of bare sandy ground where they'd done their sunbathing.

"If this goes wrong," she whispered, "you're a

good swimmer. You can distance him. He'd go
through the woods."

"You?"

"Yeah. Maybe so can I." She motioned toward the
high bank. "Stay over there. Where he can't see you."

In college she'd dated a man who threw the hammer. He wasn't close to Olympic material but he was
pretty good and he'd shown her some of the moves.
She'd done it a couple of times. This wasn't the
same, you couldn't whirl it overhead, but the principle held.

She moved in as close to the bank as possible, still
allowing for the right trajectory, and rested the axe
head at full extension, the length of the handle and
the length of her arm forming a straight line back toward the water. She faced the bank, knees bent, right
leg leading. It would be the motion of her body and
the weight of the axe head that would give her speed
and distance, not her shoulder.

She'd get one shot. He'd have plenty.

She glanced at Caroline. Caroline was okay. Out
of the way. The grass grew high there. He wouldn't
see her.

It seemed to be a long time waiting.

She concentrated on her balance, on the weight
behind her.

She heard him at their tent. Pulling back the flap.
Get ready.

She felt the adrenaline racing.

She took a breath and held it, adjusted her stance.
Calm, she thought, calm down.

Above her a twig snapped.

Then she saw him, head and shoulders appearing at once over the grass at the rim of the incline, peering out for a moment over the pond before his eyes began to shift down to her and she whirled, spun full-circle once and then halfway around again, her balance very good until just the last moment and then knowing that she'd lost it, trying to correct.

The crossbow was up and pointing at her as she let the axe fly. She watched it tumble up and saw it hit him crosswise across the midsection but it was the handle, not the axe head. The axe head grazed the crossbow and the dart flew away.

Not enough.

She hit the water just as Caroline did and for a moment before she surfaced she could see her there beside her. Then the water got muddier and darker and Michelle lost track of her.

She was using her legs and feet mostly, the heavy shoes dragging at her, her right hand useless, feeling like a white-hot ball of flame, the left arm stiffening quickly so that it was almost useless too as she stroked except to guide her. She felt her shoulder burning, her cheek burning where the dog had ripped her. Everything open now, she could tell, bleeding into the water. And it was slow, terribly slow. She thought that Caroline must be ahead of her. She hoped she was.

She surfaced again, took a breath and went under, not knowing if she'd damaged the man's bow but assuming the worst, assuming he'd reloaded by now and that if she stayed up top he could fire at her from the banks, hoping Caroline had sense enough to do the same. The jeans, the torn cotton shirt weighed heavy on her. She held her breath until she could hold it no longer and then surfaced, opening her eyes. She was more than halfway to the shore but the distance seemed immense. She dove again, kicking, squirming through the water. She surfaced once more and there was Caroline, maybe ten feet ahead of her, going down and under.

Her lungs were bursting. Why was it so *slow?*

Go past it, she thought. Past the pain.

She threw her arms ahead of her and forced herself to stroke, teeth clenched tight against the spreading pain, distilling pain into power, not caring for the pain, screw it, contempt for the pain. She pulled and pulled again, sensing that she was close now. Her head bumped something in front of her that was dark and sodden and she pulled herself around it.

She surfaced.

She stood there gasping, half out of the water, staggering toward the far shore. She saw Caroline just ahead of her, dragging herself up.

She saw her naked back and shoulders.

She saw what covered them.

Then Caroline turned around.

Michelle looked at her once and screamed.

CHAPTER FORTY-THREE

What? What was it? thought Caroline.

Michelle was screaming

She whirled to look for the man but the man wasn't there. Wasn't anywhere around them.

What then?

The scream ran down to a low trembling sound that was so unlike Michelle, so unlike anything she'd ever heard before it sent a chill skittering through her. *Somebody walking on my grave.*

She looked at Michelle. Staring back at her wide-eyed.

Something's on her, she thought.

Arms and shoulders. Neck. Dirt. The water's dirty. *Dirt on her cheek where the wound's opened up again.* Bad, open to infection. She saw her shirt pink with blood, plastered over her breasts and stomach, torn down the side. *Some dirt there too.* Clumps of it. Pond scum.

But nothing to scream about.

She's looking at *me.*

Why?

She felt something move on her face directly under her eye and brushed it off.

It wouldn't come away.

She brushed it again and felt the resistance there and that was when she saw them.

On her arms, on her hand. Everywhere.

Leeches.

She looked down over her breasts and saw them fastened to her down to her naked belly and a scream choked off into a shuddering sob inside her.

Black glistening worms that sucked and bit and crawled.

Some of them were moving.

She looked at Michelle and saw that it was not dirt, that she was covered with them too, that she knew it now and was staggering back into the water, staring at herself, staggering, bumping back suddenly into the bloated heap that rolled and turned behind her, rolled faceup now, its mouth and eyes insanely open, covered with leeches, crawling with them. The green-white face of Graham, the photographer. His corpse staring up at her open-mouthed as though enraged as she looked down and around at the swollen drifting legs, the engorged body lifting, buoying up hugely and gently out of the water.

Caroline tore at the thing beneath her eye, scraped at her cheek.

Michelle screamed again and bolted from the water.

She crushed the leech with her fingers. Blood ran out of it. *His? Mine?*

She saw Michelle stop. Almost at the shoreline.

She stared behind Caroline deep into the scrub.

And Caroline saw her clearly as she broke, as the look of horror faded.

As finally she surrendered.

As they both did.

CHAPTER FORTY-FOUR

The screams. The wounded bloody women half naked in the water. The corpse behind them.

He remembered how Sprinkles lost his cherry.

The only explanation was the frustration, the constant sick fear and far too many patrols all strung together.

They were ready to crack, all of them.

It was not that they were brutal. Recruiters for the NVA would enter a ville, take the oldest papa-san there and string him to a tree, slit open his stomach, and trail his intestines along the ground. Let the pigs eat him alive while he was dying. Then they'd say, who's coming with us and who's staying?

That was brutal. Because it was planned and cold and it happened over and over.

But when they entered that girl whore's hooch he knew they were ready to kill her. Somebody was going to pay for Ragweed's dick shoved into his mouth, after all, for lopping off his head, and if he was not prepared for the torture he expected the killing. What nobody expected was how much they'd *like* it—getting even with the real flesh and blood after weeks and months of dying at the hands of shadows.

So that when Doc found the trapdoor in the hooch's floor and the dink let go with his AK-47 they were definitely ready for more of the same. The dink didn't stand a chance. Semple, Doc, Lee, Henderson, and Sprinkles had all opened up on him. When they finished the dink's head was mush on a stumpy neck and the walls of the hole were dripping with him.

He never did find out who started up outside. Maybe Clemons. Clemons had gone out after finishing with the girl and it could have been him. But whoever it was everybody else got into it pretty quickly. Even as they ran out of the hooch villagers were scattering and the guys were chasing them, M16s on full rock 'n' roll. Mad Minute.

It was fast and wild after that and memory came only in flashes. Part of him thought they were under attack, that there were more VC in the ville other than the two they'd found. Part of him knew damn well that wasn't true, that nobody was busting caps back at him—and that part didn't care. Two VC were all they needed to finally kick some ass. And they did.

He remembered chasing a guy around the side of a hooch, shooting him in the legs to bring him down and then wasting him with one round to the head

He remembered Henderson with the M16 grenade launcher, the thumper, dropping them indiscriminately into hooches and, once at least, into a group of people. They were bunched up, hands in the air, surrendering. *Chu Hoi!* Women and children, mostly. A few men. Maybe ten in all. The grenade landed in the middle of them, just about dead center. You heard screams and then the explosion and then the whole field turned suddenly red, pieces of bodies flying like shrapnel. "Just watering the lawn," said Henderson.

He remembered seeing Clemons pull a small pretty teenage girl into one of the hooches. The girl was yelling and crying. At the time Lee was chasing somebody but the guy disappeared somewhere into the paddies so about five minutes later he was moving back the way he came.

He passed the hooch just as Clemons was coming out again.

Just in time to see him pull the pin and toss the grenade in.

He saw a really tiny kid come over to a pile of bodies and lift the hand of somebody among the dead. Mother? Father? Whoever it was the kid was crying. Thirty meters away one of the guys—it could have been Clemons again, from where Lee was he couldn't be sure—somebody dropped to his knees, aimed, and wasted the kid with a single shot.

He remembered seeing Sprinkles chasing some old papa-san, whooping like a cowboy. Out of his skull, nuts, firing into the air. Sprinkles no less. His cherry.

He wasn't proud of what he'd done that day.

For one thing he'd shot a teenage boy.

You killed kids young in Nam because kids learned killing young—the NVA was full of them—but this was different. The boy was on his knees clutching his arm. His arm was shredded halfway to the elbow.

He couldn't have hurt a fly by then. But Lee put a burst into him anyway. Because he was there. Because he was a dink.

None of them were proud. But mostly they seemed to understand that they'd gone crazy for a while that day, that killing was a sickness sometimes and there was nothing else you could call it, and they seemed to be able to forgive themselves a little.

Not Sprinkles.

Lee knew why.

He'd been running back past the paddies again when he heard the screaming.

The grass was high so he was moving cautiously, slowly, and he could still hear plenty of firing going on behind him, it wasn't over yet by a long shot and the craziness was well and truly on them. He parted the grasses in front of him with the M16. He'd been hearing the screaming and it sounded like at least two voices, both of them Vietnamese, but now, suddenly, he heard a blurt of fire and there were definitely three voices, clearly three, two of them wailing and one pitched higher, screeching in agony.

He pushed through the grass and looked out into the paddies and there was Sprinkles, standing in the water, holding the M16 in his hand and pointing it at the pair of women who pleaded with him desperately to release the girl he was holding around the waist with the other hand.

He guessed that the younger woman was the girl's sister, the older one her mother. Both of them had been wounded and the mother was bad. She was barely able to stand. Through the dirty black pajamas a blacker stain was spreading so big and fast that she must have been holding in her guts with her hands. Still she pleaded. A tiny, mournful chattering.

The girl had her back to Sprinkles. She was naked. She was screaming. At the most she was five years old.

And Sprinkles, grinning insanely, standing knee-deep in the rice paddies, was about to come inside her.

Lee watched unnoticed. It never occurred to him to stop it. Sometimes, now, he wondered why.

When he was finished Sprinkles set the girl down gently in the water. It was strange. She didn't move. She didn't run to her mother or sister. Nor did they go to her. The mother seemed to sigh and rest herself back, half in the water and halfway out, resting back against the ground and bleeding into the muck. The sister just looked down as though ashamed. And the girl lay floating on her belly, not even paddling, her face empty as only a child's can be and streaked with tears.

Sprinkles, Lee thought, looked like a dazed bull. I don't even know this man, he thought.

He watched him tuck himself back into his fatigues and look around at the three of them. Nobody met his eyes.

Blankly, almost casually, he put the gun to the back of the little girl's head and fired. The girl went under and surfaced quickly in a spreading cloud of red.

The sister started but never looked up.

The mother just seemed to let go and sank deeper into the water.

Quietly, Lee moved away.

The next night Sprinkles was dead and Lee lay under him all night long till morning.

He looked at the women now and it was so damn
close he almost had to laugh.

"Fuck it," he said. And then he did laugh.

He shouldered the crossbow and turned and
walked off into the woods.

Chapter Forty-five

Kelsey watched the man move past him searching through the grass and scrub.

It was like he wasn't even there. Boots passing by so close to him he could see the wear on the laces.

He couldn't believe that they were dead. Caroline and Michelle. Not both of them. He couldn't connect to it. It was too much to think about so he didn't even try and all he did was watch the man work an orderly circular pattern through the scrub.

He was calm. It would be all right to die now. He'd sorted through his feelings about what his life had been with an unaccustomed thoroughness lying there in the grass because there was nothing left to do but that and see if he was ready, and it surprised him to find it wanting in no respects at all. He'd left a few things behind. Not much but a little. He'd loved and been loved with more luck and courage than he suspected most men would claim. He doubted that there was a whole lot more to life than that. At least for him it seemed to make the difference. He didn't want to die but he knew he could die now without regretting everything.

All this worrying, he thought. This and that.

He found it a little strange that it was easier for him to relinquish a life he judged good and full than it would have been had he lived it poorly but it was an irony that made sense to him and one he accepted.

It was only hard to believe that they were dead.

He would have thought he'd know it somehow. The exact time. He realized he'd come to expect as much. So much waste, he thought. All you people poorer now.

He watched the man reach into the brush and find the shotgun.

He broke it open, inspected the chamber and snapped it shut.

Do it neatly, he thought. The way I did your dog.

The man stood there a moment squinting into the sun. Then he turned and glanced at Kelsey. He walked over.

Kelsey looked up at him but the man's face was lost in the glare of sunlight. He gestured with the shotgun.

"Mind if I borrow this?"

Kelsey just looked at him. *What's he saying here?*

"I don't think you do."

He began to walk away. "Don't worry," he said. "They'll be coming for you. They're okay."

Kelsey felt something fill and lift suddenly in his chest. The man stopped and turned.

"Here."

He tossed something into Kelsey's lap. A round flat piece of plastic and metal. The ignition rotor.

"You know what day today is?" asked the man.

"I . . . it's Sunday."

He nodded. He stared at Kelsey a moment, then tipped the shotgun toward him.

"Welcome Home," he said.

And then he walked away.

It was nice out here among the trees. The stream was flowing cool and clear. There was a good steady breeze. He dipped his hand into the water, cupped it, and brought it to his mouth. He wondered why it had never occurred to him that water had a taste before.

It tasted like earth and sky.

He drank again.

He wasn't far away. They'd find him.

It was a good place.

You see? he thought. I'm keeping my promise to you, Alma. I told you it would never be you. That it would never be.

I love you too much for that. And I love the boy.

He pictured them clearly. He pictured the dog. He even pictured a little house in Ellsworth, New Hampshire, he'd thought of buying once and fixing up for them. The house was over a hundred and fifty years old. He could have got it cheap. It would have been nice for the boy.

He thought about McCann. McCann would have a widow now.

Christ! The mind was a lonely place.

He drank. Clean clear water. *Earth and sky*.

Don't call him *the boy*, he thought. Call him Lee Jr. The dog was Pavlov. Funny but I never had any trouble with Alma.

He tilted the shotgun toward his lips, aware of their sudden warmth as they touched the barrel.

EPILOGUE

Caroline finished stacking the dishes in the dishwasher tray, closed the door and turned it on. The machine made a small whirring sound. It was the quietest dishwasher she'd ever heard. She reminded herself again to replace the one in Bel Air with another just like it.

She rinsed and dried her hands, took her glass of Bordeaux off the counter and walked the long barn-board corridor into the living room.

Michelle had a fire going. She was sitting on a rug in front of it sipping tea, her back to the couch. In another month or so she was going to have trouble sitting like that no matter how strong she stayed from the exercises. According to the sonogram it was a boy and it looked to Caroline like it was going to be a big one. She'd studied up,

"Done," she said and sat down on the couch. Michelle smiled at her. "I hate doing dishes. But that dinner of yours was worth it. Of course I also hate it that you cook better than I do."

"Caroline. You don't cook. You never cook."

"I know. I hate it anyway. How're we doing?"

Mich laughed. "We're fine."

Caroline settled back and sipped her drink. She was aware that she was chattering. It was unlike her. She saw now that there were two fires—one in the fireplace and one reflected in the wall-sized window. The Arizona night was moonless and filled with stars.

"The same kind of night," she said. "Remember?"

"I remember."

"I think of Alan."

She wondered if she'd had enough drinks for this. She wasn't sure. But she knew she wanted it. It had been bothering her for a long time now—ever since Mich had invited her to the ranch to help with the baby, and that had been months already.

The timing was good too, with Kelsey asleep upstairs and just the two of them together. Kelsey knew all about it already and he'd urged her to discuss it. So it wasn't that. It was just that this was private between them.

She took another sip of Dutch courage. Could you say that of a pretty fair Bordeaux?

"Mich?"

"Mmmm?"

To be exact it had bothered her ever since the night Mich told her she'd decided to go ahead and have the baby. She was going to be out of modeling for a while in any case, she said. Her hand was never going to be the same but her face would heal again eventually, even if it took some surgery, so she'd work again. Still she had time now. And she wanted it. She really did. She wanted it very much.

If Caroline would help her. There were still a lot

of things she needed to do that had nothing to do with modeling. So she would want and need help with a child.

The point was, she said, how would a kid be with two mothers?

Confused, said Caroline. Then she cried.

Michelle had laughed. We can handle it.

Kelsey'd been delighted.

But she'd felt guilty ever since.

She put her glass down on the table.

Might as well, she thought. It was only getting harder.

"Back in the woods that first day. Before . . . when I first knew you were pregnant. We'd just set up the abortion, you know?"

"Mmmm."

"I was thinking of doing something . . . really terrible."

"What was that?"

She felt her eyes pool up and quickly shook it off. Get on with it, she thought. No plays for sympathy.

"I was thinking of telling the papers."

She waited to let that sink in. Mich sipped her tea.

"To screw you," she said. "I was seriously thinking about it, Mich."

Michelle put down her teacup and looked at her thoughtfully.

"No, you weren't," she said. She smiled and took her hand. And Caroline felt the smooth scar tissue, the delicate reconstruction within.

"Not seriously," she said. "I don't buy that for a minute."

She let herself go then and began to cry, because of course it was true, she never would have.

She didn't bother with the bastards anymore, no more, she was better than that, and she never would have.

The fire crackled.

Upstairs Kelsey was dreaming.

In the dream he was out in the woods again and it was night and there was no moon, but he was alone this time, it was different in that one respect from some of the other dreams and it was worse, much worse than being with Alan or Ross or Graham, he was alone and carrying a shotgun, lunging.

He stepped over a log on the forest floor and saw that it was a man's body. He stepped over another and that was a body too. He recognized neither man but naturally he wouldn't, they were lying facedown exactly as he'd shot them, exactly as he'd watched them fall. He was endowed with the perfect night-vision of the practiced hunter and he was dangerous now in the blackness of a moonless, starless night. He was alone, insane.

Hunting.

He woke up screaming.

A pair of arms slid gently around him.

The arms were soft—their touch very firm. It was dark in his room, as dark as it was in the dream, and at first he didn't know whose they were, which woman they belonged to.

It didn't matter.

AFTERWORD

Thomas Tessier

Ah, now wasn't that a thoroughly satisfying read? A well-constructed novel with deftly drawn, convincing characters. A plot that advances with an exquisite sense of timing, steadily escalating tension and volcanic eruptions of violence. Oh yes, let us quickly agree that Jack Ketchum's *Cover* is a fine adventure indeed, an outdoors Gothic thriller that takes us on a wild ride and ends up hauling us through a very tight wringer. It is as effective as a hard punch in the throat.

But something is different with this book—and you know what I mean. Where's that cozy afterglow we're used to experiencing at the conclusion of a good entertainment? Where is the lingering tingle of vicarious pleasure that tells us our readerly desires have been fulfilled? The author does not entirely deny us these humble rewards, but the afterglow is decidedly brief and accompanied by a sense of chill in the air, while the tingle is rather subdued.

If you already know this man's work, you know that his very special gift is to create a floating bubble of unease within us. Like the air bubble in a carpenter's level, it's an important indicator—but we can

303

never quite get it, or ourselves, back on center again. This insistent little bubble subtly alters our intellectual, emotional and even spiritual understanding of who we are and the world in which we live. I wish I could tell you to relax because the bubble is harmless and will dissolve, but I honestly can't. I'd like to be able to tell you to forget about it—but you probably won't. Nor should you.

Because Jack Ketchum is not just a natural-born storyteller, a jolly wicked entertainer and a highly skilled craftsman—he is all of that, and more. He is a real writer, by which I mean that his work inevitably leads us to glimpses of the truth about ourselves, the kind of inner truth that only fiction of high quality can reveal. No, this truth does not set us free, alas. But in some small, vital way it does help, and we can hardly ask more of any human art.

Cover was his third novel, and it confirmed the powerful promise he had shown in *Off Season* and *Hide and Seek*. Once again he sets up a titanic struggle between people who find themselves thrown together in a lonely place—lonely in both a geographic and a psychic sense. We're familiar with these confrontations, at least as far back as James Dickey's *Deliverance*. Some characters will live, some will die horribly, and for the survivors life will never be quite the same. This is a path of literature that is almost Biblical in the simplicity and the ultimate vastness of its vision. For the reader, it's quite irresistible.

But what Jack Ketchum gives us is really a kind of anti-*Deliverance*, which I find much more disturbing and satisfying. In the Dickey novel, a few recognizable,

fairly normal American businessmen venture fool-
ishly into a stretch of wilderness where they become
the targets of some savage locals and must fight their
way back to civilization. It is a highly effective entertainment, it was a bestselling book and a very successful movie—and yet, for me at least, *Deliverance* has
never had any special resonance. There is a tedious
machismo at the heart of it, and also the clear impli-
cation that the primitive locals really don't have anything to do with the rest of us and our world. They
are the residue of the dim past, genetic throwbacks
hanging on in remote woodsy pestholes.

Jack Ketchum has bigger fish to fry. When he takes
us into the woods we're really going to find out why
our mothers warned us to stay away from there. In
Off Season, his cunning retelling of the old Scottish
tale of Sawney Bean, relocated on the scenic coast of
Maine, he shows us the flip side of the American family, and it's a truly nightmarish vision—one we can-
not shrug off or wish away. Ketchum found his stroke
in his first at-bat, and this powerful novel immediately made me a reader of his for life.

A later novel, *The Girl Next Door,* contains passages
that are very nearly unbearable to read, but by then the
author has us firmly in his grip, and when he pulls the
curtain back it is impossible for us not to peer inside.
One of the sad and scary things we see here is that it
isn't necessary to travel any distance from home to find
the woods—they're all around us, we live in them.

Cover is richer in its characterizations, in its humor
and insights, structure, and most of all in its emotional
complexity. But for all of that, it sacrifices nothing in

momentum and force. We can both like and dislike the small group of well-off Angelenos who set out for a pleasant weekend in the woods, and in no time at all we feel we know them as real people. They're all smart and mostly successful, but also rather pampered and perhaps dangerously self-centered. The curious marriage and thorny personal relationships of Bernard Kelsey, a successful novelist, serve as an unusual but fitting counterpoint to the main narrative.

The monster they meet is Lee Moravian, a severely damaged Vietnam vet who has retreated from the world and wants nothing more than to be left alone, to tend his marijuana patch, to hold off his inner ghosts and somehow get through the rest of his ill-fated life. In short, he's one of us, one of ours—our brother, our son, the kid next door who grew up, who we sent to hell, and who brought it back home to us. In such a confrontation we can hardly bear to take sides, since we are both sides. It is a tribute to the author's artistry that he refuses to give us the formulaic Vietnam vet as either a crazed maniac or an innocent victim to be pitied at arm's length. Moravian has some of both in him, naturally, but there is much more to him than that. Life is not simple, and Jack Ketchum leads us again and again to the point where we have to deal with that singular fact.

Cover is a particular favorite of mine among his works. In it you can see his vision widening, his reach extending, his art unfolding almost effortlessly. He takes us where we don't want to go, to see what we don't want to see. He knows it is necessary—this, after all, is what real fiction does. We meet Grendel—and oh, how well we recognize him. Ketchum is a master at confounding the reader's expectations, so the story plays out in ways we never anticipate and which are all the more convincing for that. We may think we understand what is happening, but we keep learning that our grasp is shaky at best.

The first readers who noticed Jack Ketchum were horror fans, because that is how his work was marketed. Call it horror or psychological horror, suspense or thriller, call it even dark suspense—if you must. To me, this is literature that is a part of, and an honorable addition to, the long tradition of the true Gothic, which is not only alive and well but is an especially apt and vibrant form in our era. Gothic fiction is amazingly flexible and adaptable, ranging from intense claustrophobic chamber drama to the grand high opera of the supernatural. You only have to think about the varied works of authors as different as Peter Straub, Stephen King, Joyce Carol Oates and Patrick McGrath (to name but four of many) to realize how great the possibilities are.

Among them, Jack Ketchum's voice is unique and unmistakable (I almost forgot to mention that his descriptions of the natural world are dazzling, some of the best we've had since Hemingway and Algernon Blackwood). If his work has not yet attracted all the attention it deserves, that may be due to the fact that his vision of people and life in this world is uncompromising in its honesty, and that's not to everybody's taste. Too bad—it's their loss. He is a deeply American author with an unflinching gaze, and yet there is a kind of bleak tenderness at the heart of his work that I find very moving.

Reading any of Ketchum's novels is a remarkable experience. You have the sense of naughty pleasure that any good summer beach thriller offers, the excitement and action, the rapid pace and engaging story. But you also feel sweatier, and much more exhausted on the inside, in some way both humbled and exalted. Believe me, that's good, very good, and you won't find it in any beach book. Only writing of a much higher level can bring us such precious gifts.

For which, my last word after is: Thanks.

Horror in Culture & Entertainment
RUE MORGUE

MAGAZINE

VISIT OUR WEBSITE:
RUE-MORGUE.COM

GET FREE BOOKS!

You can have the best fiction delivered to your door for less than what you'd pay in a bookstore or online. Sign up for one of our book clubs today, and we'll send you *FREE* BOOKS* just for trying it out... **with no obligation to buy, ever!**

As a member of the Leisure Horror Book Club, you'll receive books by authors such as **RICHARD LAYMON, JACK KETCHUM, JOHN SKIPP, BRIAN KEENE** and many more.

As a book club member you also receive the following special benefits:
- **30% off all orders!**
- **Exclusive access to special discounts!**
- **Convenient home delivery and 10 days to return any books you don't want to keep.**

Visit **www.dorchesterpub.com**
or call **1-800-481-9191**

There is no minimum number of books to buy, and you may cancel membership at any time.
*Please include $2.00 for shipping and handling.